Someone Like U

WILLIAM SWEENEY

Someone Like U

TATE PUBLISHING
AND ENTERPRISES, LLC

Published by Tate Publishing & Enterprises, LLC
127 E. Trade Center Terrace | Mustang, Oklahoma 73064 USA
1.888.361.9473 | www.tatepublishing.com

Tate Publishing is committed to excellence in the publishing industry. The company reflects the philosophy established by the founders, based on Psalm 68:11,
"The Lord gave the word and great was the company of those who published it."

Cover design by Gian Philipp Rufin
Interior design by Jake Muelle

Published in the United States of America

ISBN: 978-1-63449-800-5
Fiction / Romance / Contemporary
15.03.09

How does a conversation begin? Prelude, accident, curiosity, or destiny.

An impromptu chat was the beginning of the relationship between Lee and Bill. Their eyes caught up to each other through a mundane afternoon bunch of shoppers. An emotional surge was just enough for him to throw out a curve—even though she sensed it was coming. A burst of courage coupled with anticipation created a unique conversation about something so ordinary.

A grin

"Are you the actress they told me about?

Letting go

"No, I'm not! Funny you asked—why?

Proclaiming

"I thought you were the one."

Conversations—faint ones, incomplete, forgotten, nearby, old and missing ones—connect two worlds of a writer. Flowing back and forth between material and spiritual, a conversation is a path to rambling, wandering, discovery, and escaping. Who started this conversation? Was this conversation happening before they met? Was Lee part of the physical or spiritual? What did they both see just before meeting?

Was the conversation a way to feel—what was missing?

Contents

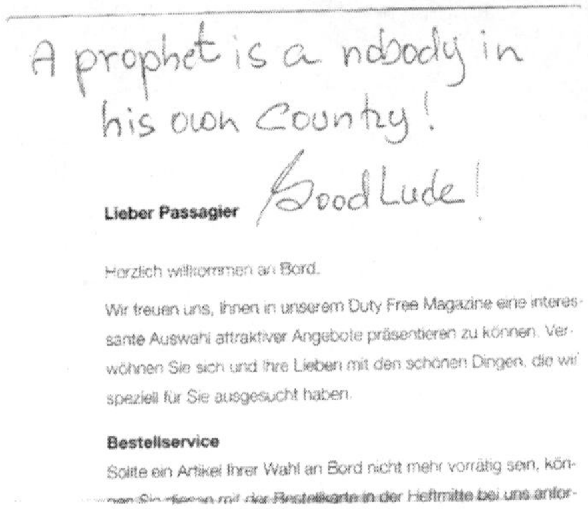

A prophet is a nobody in his own country!

Good Lude!

Lieber Passagier

Herzlich willkommen an Bord.

Wir freuen uns, Ihnen in unserem Duty Free Magazine eine interessante Auswahl attraktiver Angebote präsentieren zu können. Verwöhnen Sie sich und Ihre Lieben mit den schönen Dingen, die wir speziell für Sie ausgesucht haben.

Bestellservice

Sollte ein Artikel Ihrer Wahl an Bord nicht mehr vorrätig sein, können Sie diesen mit der Bestellkarte in der Heftmitte bei uns anfor-

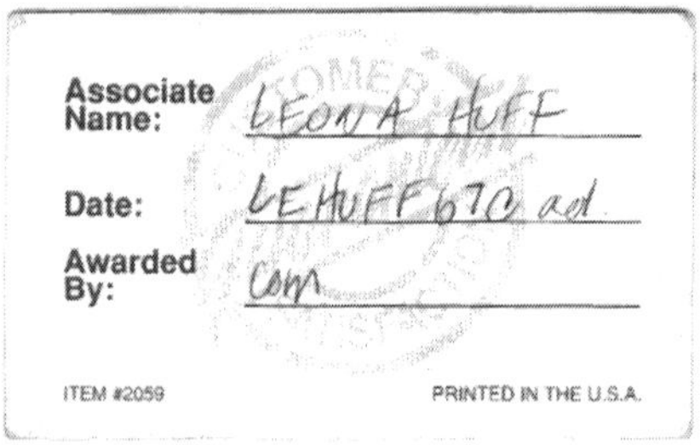

Associate Name: LEONA HUFF

Date: LEHUFF670 aol

Awarded By: com

ITEM #2059 PRINTED IN THE U.S.A.

A prophet is a nobody in his own country!

Good Lude!

The Hookup

Sub: Re: meeting up
Date: 12/08/99:18:34 AM Eastern Standard Time
From: LEHUFF67
To: NYCBlackout

Bill,

I have just printed out *Le Edison Effect*, your new screen play. I'm going to read it today. I agree it was odd the way in which we met. I have recently decided to commit myself to pursuing writing. So to meet a writer in such a random place and way is what is that? Perhaps I am so focused on my goal, and you are the same with your work, that we created meeting.

Since you have shared your work with me, I shall send you my latest complete piece. I did not edit it and did not have an editor, so there are a few typos. It's nothing egregious, but they exist.

This piece, *an unabridged essay on The Way I See 'IT'* is directed to a man/child I met in Italy. It is a commentary on life as we know it at the end of the 20th century and life as it has been for centuries.

Life is too short to not be direct and honest. Otherwise, time is lost. And life is made complicated. I come from a long line of tough, single-minded. Get the job done, do it right the first time. And move on to the next task. No nonsense. I don't have time for nonsense. I find solace in nature. Like Emily Dickinson's "A Song of Sonnet."

So I think I will have to e-mail the essay separately, forward it to you. Let me know what you think. I will contact you as soon as I have a chance to read *Le Edison Effect.*

How is it that you have written about Louisiana? Did you spend time there? I am really looking forward to reading that piece.

Take care.

Sub: Understanding
Date: 12/09/99
From: LEHUFF67
To: NYCBlackout

Bill,

As I am without a lot of food in my stomach, my mind finds itself overloaded by all of your thoughts. A lot to process. What was I feeling when I did what? Share that with you or write it? Looking for a mirage? No. Validation.

Love. Love. Love. We hate so much trouble, Americans with love. I, however, am finished with trouble. Completely. I have decided. I think that when there is love, there is something created and manifested. Love can foster creativity, genius. You name it. I know. I saw it. I experienced it. I was there. It happens.

How is it that I find people? They find me, who is not constrained by the religion of the collective? Who believe in reincarnation and past lives? It is no accident. I wonder who is making it happen. It must be me. Could be somebody else, like you? It happens. I'm looking for answers from the great beyond.

You know, I too have friends in the woods, fairies, they are. I am thinking that although I am still very young, I might have a great many of the answers. Not all. I must return to Italy. There must be in grade school a class where all the English words you need—to talk the talk and remember, poetically, romantically—are taught to Italian men. Or it could be the obvious source. He would say the most beautiful things, and the next day. I knew in the pit of my stomach that he was false so, what do you do?

It depends on what you want. But when you make a choice like that, in such a situation, you always sell yourself short. And then, it gets to be a game of kill or be killed. And that always takes way too much energy, more than it's worth. It is indeed about my voice. Some days I'm 50, some days I'm 80. I have lived and died so many times, I can't tell you.

I had a Renaissance of my own while in Italy. Florence, I think it was. I have a new life. This is the one. I'm pretty sure. There is so much to do. I can hardly find time to sleep. I have yet to read *Le Edison Effect*. What a good editor I have turned out to be!

I'll see you tomorrow between 3 and 4.

Take care.

Peace is with you, as well.

Lee

Sub: Hoping…
Date: 12/09/99 11:46:07 PM Eastern Standard Time
From: NYC blackout
To: LEHUFF67

Hi,

It was so good of you to come by today, to pick up the script. Really, it was cool to share symbols of nature, moss, & incense. I was so glad to see you. Yet I felt a scary glimpse from your heart—like you didn't want to accept them.

Wisdom allows you to confirm that there are no mistakes, only hiccups. I have no hidden agenda in writing back to you, or talking to you. In Italy, it was a chance to go for the top, an echelon. If you were to meet someone tomorrow and get swept off your feet, and you're in simpatico, I'd be happy for you. I'd be one of those from a distance that would be wishing you well, serenity. Happiness. A different kind of fullness that you've worked for and on so long. Some kind of joy, partners up with your dream.

I'm always struggling when people label life as a box of cereal. Life is replete with idiosyncrasies, ups and downs, wins and losses. If you can own up to a mistake, the thing to do is acknowledge it. Keep moving on up to your goals and dreams. If you were to open up to me— like a flower in spring, responding to bright sun light—I'm open to sensing more of you. I like listening to you. I'm interested in free will. What keeps me centered is patience. The whole banana. I want to learn more about being patient.

While in Europe, I traveled with a girl friend (Amy) to a small town in Central Sweden. We went by train to eat dinner with her aunt and uncle. It's been so long. I can't remember their names. All I remember is their spirit. Local cheeses and smoked salmon were excellent. The beers were to die for. User-friendly too. After eating, I started clearing the table. Somewhat like a bird coming from behind a tall oak tree, her uncle shouted out in broken Swedish/English, "You're kind." I responded, "I'm trying to learn what kindness is—how it feels to be kind."

What are you asking for? Do we understand consequences? Do we want to accept different? How do you want to move? Why go over there?

Until I hear from you, you have my warm wishes.

Bill

Old Car with Vines growing and leaves Photograph

Peeling Back

Sub: Understanding!!!!
Date: 12/10/999:56:02 PM Eastern Standard time
From: NYC blackout
To: LEHUFF67

Hi,

I'm beginning to understand your pain, your angst, your toughness, your courage, your strengths, and your vulnerability—not that I know much about them. But I'm beginning to understand them, and I wanted you to know that. I accept you not only for where you are, but where you want to be.

Today was a day full of trouble and doubts. Mainly, it was battling the cold and searching for some strength to continue a film project losing its soul. No, I didn't have the strength to play tennis. I spent a lot of time sweating and coughing all day. It was if something wanted to come out, and my resistance was moving aside. I felt lighter and more confident.

Then I called London. Martin was shopping and driving around London. Later on, we talked about two hours later between my naps. During the conversation, he agreed to e-mail me a provisional 40% budget commitment letter on Monday and a standard sales agent agreement, which we need to complete prior to financing. I have an aversion to all the financing schemes. They suck.

No doubt, I like the creating process. It's pretty cool. Visualizing a story. Feeling out a character. Letting a character speak to me, like she or he speaks—not my language, but their own twinge. I almost forgot to ask, what's the difference between jealousy and envy? I just got through reading your e-mail of 12/8/99. The more I read what you write, the more I realize you're better than where you are in life. You are a walking gold mine. Maybe going back to Italy will allow you an opportunity to make that happen.

In writing, critics and experts agree that you should write about what you know. You asked me if had gone to Rome or to Louisiana. I've lived in Lake Charles. My son, Adam, was born in Lake Charles so he's a Cajun at heart. I respect Edwin Edwards, although it appears he's a crook. But has he done some good for the people? Too bad he along with the other dudes in office want to fill their pockets first and then the people get the crumbs. Emerald is one of my favorite chefs to watch. He's actually Cajun Portuguese, but I love his dramatic take on little things like garlic cloves and spices. His recipes are so simple to make. I get off on cooking, making a mess in the kitchen and living to tell about it. Actually, I cook a lot. Italian and Mexican are my favorites. If you want to know, I have never met a bowl of pasta I didn't like.

I've been to Rome, Italy, twice and was blown away. It was a scene—the American Gringo seeing pay dirt, without enough money to take a bite. I went over with a neat story idea, but nothing else to go along with it—not a stranger in paradise, but a bum in wonderland. I couldn't speak the lingo, and I really had no idea of where or who to turn to. Confusion ruled the day. I was looking for money and trying to sign an actress.

Don't misunderstand me. It has a lot to do with a woman's inner energy, intuition, sensitivity, softness, and wisdom. I'm bewildered by a certain look from a stranger. I get excited where I'm in touch with madness. Balancing the ship is a woman's unique way of viewing the world—crazy different. I'm particularly drawn to how a woman thinks and ponders. I'm into instincts. I once read that it's harder to think, than to do. I stand accused of thinking too much.

I've been in Atlanta since 1992, and I'm ready to leave. Divorced in 1991. I came here from Dallas, TX. I chose to live alone due to my art process. Writing. I'm moody. Sometimes when I'm working on a story, I get swooped up in a magic ball of wonderment—not knowing, unsure, but motivated to keep going, to find out. It's so heavy that I don't recognize anything or anybody around me. As I get near a turing point of discovery, I wouldn't mind sharing a revelation with someone else.

I have this notion that my partner was in Europe somewhere. I've had a letter correspondence with a girl in Munich for almost two years, and we only knew a few things about each other. But there were times when I thought I knew a lot about her. Was that a paradox? How can you feel comfortable with somebody you haven't seen in two years?

I like it when it's quiet. My apartment is quiet except when I turn the music on. The sound is somewhere between soft and loud. I have no TV. It's a waste of energy, yet I'm into technology because it's connected to intelligence.

So writing has been a part of me since college. College newspaper. An Army Magazine. Creative Loafing. Atlanta Black Business Monthly. Atlanta Press and KAOS Films. I think KAOS has something to do with destiny in Greek—that's why I choose the name.

Writing allows me to express an idea. A feeling. Without explanations, like in everyday conversations. You have to explain yourself over and over. Clarity.

The naked eye, an edge of your intuition, spots an image, an inkling. You really don't know what it is or even what it means. Gradually, you start leaning toward curiosity—a chance to embrace hysteria. What's interesting is that you have a chance to connect up to a peculiar feeling again. Another thing is that it almost grabs you, as if it is already there. You wander around.

When you meet a stranger, the first thing that you feel is fear. You don't know what to say, because you don't know who you're talking to. You're communicating an idea to an unknown. Somebody you just meet. The twist is in persuading them to believe you. That is a challenge. I'm looking to learn more about confidence.

For real, I'm my own worst critic. I'll share this with you about writing and your writing. Do not let me repeat; do not listen to me about your writing. As a matter of fact, don't listen to anyone else about your writing.

Wrap your brain around your feelings and thoughts. Accept a thought that you could be on to something. Understand what you want to write about. Do your due diligence. Research, homework, interviews. Spend time at the library and courthouse records. Dig into and Google and MSN.

Now you're going from standing around to movement. Before you leave the station, check your gut. Yeah it's time to get going. This story don't belong to mom, pop, granddad, or grandma. It's good to have family to encourage you—to cheer you up, when you're down. Even little boys need encouragement. At the end of the day, you're left alone with your story.

You feel a story, as a baby in a woman's belly. There's a pregnancy. Incubation. A unique opportunity for another life, setting foot on earth—a sudden rush to see if it's a boy or a girl. Medical tests. Doctor visits. Blood pressure ups and down, all over the map. Staying off your feet. Baby shower. Weight fluctuations. A ton of gifts from folks you didn't know, before you got pregnant. So many, a young mother might not know what to do with it. Then, after nine months or so—a baby comes out.

Could this be a similar feeling you get as you start out on your own? Searching your gut, looking for a new port, trying to understand an old nightmare, navigating a different destination—you were so scared to visit before?

Don't be afraid to screw your story up. It's a piece of clay formed with insights, an uneven character, empathy, vision along with wisdom. Please don't be afraid to make a mistake with your story. Any mistake is a part of learning, gaining another understanding. In life, you're always doing your best at this particular point. After the dust settles, you might discover something different that could have changed an outcome. Yet you go for what you know.

Make up your own story, and remain quiet. Protect it as a secret—a secret, known only to you. Let your feelings do the talking. You might want to let the characters speak for themselves. Two roses in a flower bed, neither tells the other one to grow.

Don't be afraid to be alone with your story. Don't forget for a minute that isolation is your "home boy." When you get to the point of criticizing your story, yourself, and your characters—remember that you're the only one criticizing.

Take it slow, now. Be kind. Be bold. Be tough. Allow your story to shape its own form, own substance—it's own flavor.

So after philosophy (804), is there something else? Get back to your computer. Start typing. Complete index cards. Make some dumb calls. Hold your head up. Check out the stars. Go for it. It will be all right.

Bill

Water Lilly Photograph

Sub: Wait a minute…
Date: 12/11/99 12:47:54 PM Eastern Standard lime
From: LEHUFF67
To: NYCblackout

Bill,

I thought I had buried the hatchet. Did I not? Am I missing, what am I missing? Let go. Let go. How do I do that? Help me. I am not defining myself; I do not need a man to define who I am. I thought, and if I am fooling myself, tell me. I was/am keeping the only thing possible alive. He can't give me what I want. I don't want what he has. But as another human being, a troubled one to be sure, there is and can be still the connection. I'm looking for more ugliness.

I'm off the game board with him in that regard. Now, in my mind, there is a fantasy. But that is a fantasy. We all need new material for daydreams. I don't know. I am holding onto him, but what is wrong with that? I am not pinning my future to his coattail. He is merely a distraction, something to think about and remember. There was the illusion of love. There were illusions of many things.

Clearly, I am not ready to let go; but in my daydream, we are not sitting together when I'm 64. In my daydream, he's seducing me. He's making me laugh and feeding me feeding me chocolate, from a spoon. His knack is whispering softly, into my ear. He is not the father of my children. He's a flame, a fling. Yes, I loved him. Did he love me back?

OK. Can't I keep the part I can keep? And still, move on and do what I need to do for myself?

Or is it that I must banish him from my mind and life as well? I am asking you because I do not have the answer.

Tell me. And I honestly did not expect anything more from him.

I know and understand his limitations. They are great and many, to be sure, but there is something about him I still want. Am I destroying myself?

Am I living somebody else's life? What am I to do? I don't know where or how or what you picked up, but perhaps, I am still fragile and weak and afraid from the hell I put myself through. I quaked, and moaned, and felt as if I was sent through.

Here's a big old hurricane. Yeah. Yeah. Yeah. I agree with the view Western Society has on love. I know all about that.

And I also know how to relate to another human being as a spiritual being. Because we are actually spiritual beings having a physical experience. I understand all of these things. But I have to protect myself.

I am a woman, living among the collective. I know love in Western Society. How do I know all you know? How do you know all I know? How many people do you meet that get it? Relax. I'm just trying to take care of myself. I don't have a choice. And there is much to protect, and if I don't do it, it won't get done.

Look. There are too many things that you, as a man, cannot understand as to the experiences of a woman. You cannot argue with that, it's clear-cut. I've just come from Rome. And there are things you simply cannot understand about what I felt and saw, and I mean, I barely got out of there alive. So it must be all of that. Hold up a minute. Relax. I'm with you. I'm sorry for the confusion and misunderstanding.

Am I not enjoying my own moments? What? I don't see it.

My view is not that you are suggesting that I change. I am trying to learn, to understand. How else am I going to get there? And have I not expressed my gratitude to you? One of us or both got the lines of communication crossed. Show me. Tell me. Teach me.

I do want a friend. I've not been offended. I am employing caution. I am only a tiny, small creature. I'm strong, I'm quick, but I am of the weaker sex. And that is the end of that. Are we clear? I hope you are well; what is the situation with the cold today?

Here's wishing joy to the fishes, in the deep blue sea. Joy to you and me.

Peace,
Lee

Rear View Mirror Photograph

Sub: Donde Esta?
Date: 12/12/9912:12:08 AM Eastern Standard lime
From: LEHUFF67
To: NYCblackout

Bill,

I thought about you a lot today. I expected to find a message. I was disappointed to find you elsewhere.

I must go fold clothes and clean the house. I'm having guests at 11. No matter what I do, think to do, the messes refuse to clean themselves up. I am always required to assist, in the same manner that I created. I can't figure how to get around that.

Here is my fortune cookie from dinner:

> You are ready to let your creative talents blossom so, what do you think about that?

Hope you are well.

Lee

Railroad Track with hanging trees

Sub: Re: Wait a minute...
Date: 12/12/9912:39:17 A M Eastern Standard lime
From: NYCblackout
To: LEHUFF67

Hola!

So you got excited about what I said. Like I was saying something that got you upset. Your experience in Italy has happened to so many other souls under different continents. And there have been people who have survived.

You could go out to a high-end party in Atlanta. Every strut you move turns heads from way across the room. Even women take notice. Then a barrel-chested dude makes his way over, rescuing you from the crowd. Sparks fly. We're talking December 12, 1999, a Sunday evening. Once you guys hook up, it would only mean you're ready for the next move.

When you fall in love, you're wallowing between hope and illusion. You're dancing to an unwritten song. Your moves come, not by design, only from gumption. Relinquishing. Handing things over. Giving up and giving in. Sharing. Offering. Allowing. You could care less, what's coming your way.

Love has many authors. Reputably, there are experts. On one hand—it's an emotion. Occasionally slipping—slightly outside a notion.

For sure, I don't know all the details about what happened over there. It's none of my business. It is ok to move beyond the question of who was right or who was wrong. Does anybody know? If they do, what part of the story are they missing?

Indeed, why does love have to be so sad?

Opportunities, like love and happiness, don't come around every day. There're folks out there who confess that it won't happen in a lifetime. Actually meeting your soul mate. Yet one imagines it might be a meeting of spirits. Unique souls uniting. One could also imagine a merging of minds. Emotions blending. Hearts coalescing. Even though they're performing different rhythms. A flowing mood, signals them over yonder. Exploring. Touching. Flying. Landing, in proximity.

Blissful. Magical like there's no time. Only destinations indicating a particular energy. Unpredictable. None predicated on what went on, in the past. None anticipating what will or should happen in the future. Escaping any kind of description from Webster's.

Our hopes, desires, and dreams are just around the corner. So both of you had this opportunity. The physical moment could be over, but the emotional moment lingers. If you could do it all over again, what would you do? It's so good for you to write about it. Now you can work on your story. Develop your writing. You've learned to release your emotions. Where is your head? What are you thinking about? The future. The past. Where do you want to go? Are you there? Are you healing? You possess a freedom to retain anything from your life. This is your choice. No approvals from mankind are required.

If you want to maintain a friendship with Mr. G, that would be right too. Mainly because you're exercising your free will. Be vigilant on what is best for you. And if you're healing, that's good. That's a process unto itself that takes time. One needs time to gather energy to regain self-respect. Generate full confidence. Become aware of the situation. If this is where you stand, it only means that you're in the process of getting things together. Why do you want to argue with me, about something so simple?

Don't forget to smell the roses. Smell an aroma. Life is very short on earth. There will be plenty of other opportunities for you to experience true romance, without armor. Yet if you want that, make yourself available.

I know a lot of people who live in the past. It is framing your whole life, on what happened five years ago. They look back, instead of forward. Is it possible to grow under this mind-set? By the way, who is your best friend?

I'm inspired from affirmations. Peter (the prophet) described them as the fruits of the Spirit: love, kindness, patience, generosity, meekness, forbearance, consideration, and peace. A stranger's affirmation feels like a confirmation.

I'm hoping this note finds you well. Healthy and in good spirits.

Peace,
Bill

Acknowledging

Sub: OK, OK, OK…OK…I get it!
Date: 12/12/993:20:33 A M Eastern Standard 1ime
From: LEHUFF67
To: NYCblackout

Bill, Bill, Bill, Bill, Bill, Bill, All right. I hear you I see it now.

Just think how long I would have gone on like this, if you had not, if it weren't for you. Thank you, my friend.

Thank you. Thank you. Thank you!

I am, as each day passes, more and more, overwhelmed by you and your thoughts and your thoughtfulness and your love. When I got to the end of your response, I cried.

I can find no words to express all that I feel. God bless you! As I sit here, I am feeling better. I must be letting go.

And actually, my head has been in the clouds for, I don't know how long. I have not been myself. What am I thinking about? I think I have not been thinking. I have been so wrapped up into all of this, which I cannot/have not been able to think. I don't know what I'd be doing. I've been clogged up; my brain has been of no use to me. What about that?

So you must know that when I got to the question. So why do you want to argue with me about something so simple? I had to get up and walk away. And I laughed out loud! That was wonderful! You got me good!

But, But, But, But, love doesn't have to be sad. And that's the point. OK. OK! So have you found your soul mate?

What if I think that if you do what you need to do for yourself, and you just go along about your way, the soul mate may drop in your lap while you're not looking? And do you mean to say that, what do you mean by high probability? I have decided to find him. That's what I want. Can't I have it? I'm tired of the dress rehearsals. I'm ready for the *big* show.

I'm picking up on The Real Bacon. I can even see The Big Enchilada. Can the rest of this now be finished? So now I know. Do I know enough to make it happen? Or is there something else I've overlooked? I don't see why I can't be perfectly happy and find that love. I can be patient. No, I really have a problem with that. Just give me something to do in the meantime. So tell me. I want to know.

Who is my best friend?

Daniel Prescott Graves is his name. We grew up together. We meet in the second grade. It was in Sister Ester's class.

We would spend hours on the phone in the sixth grade. We were tight then. In the summertime, we would have bike days. We would meet halfway and ride all day. We would go to his grandmother's house, Mama Lou, for water, it was halfway to LSU. And when a car would approach, we would tell the other, "car." We would spell it out. It had its own rhythm. High school was difficult, as it is for most. We went to separate all-girls and all-boys. I was not happy then. I don't get on well with women. It was a sorority—you had no choice but to join. Then I went to LSU. We had a *ball*! I still wonder how I finished.

Our relationship has as its usual cadence; we have had periods of years when we did not speak. But when we do speak. Again, there is never a need to; it just picks right back up. We just 2 weeks ago came out of one of those periods. That was a long one, three years. But Danny knows. He was there. He's in all of my stories.

They are silly stories. We monkey around a lot. He picks on me. He tells stories on me. He can be relentless. He knows all the buttons and takes great joy in twisting them.

Danny, Danny, Danny. I used to, whenever some trivial, silly thing that would go wrong, I would always say, "It's Danny's fault!"

And then he would always buy into it. Or act like he was, anyway. I use to have this answering machine that would record the conversation if it picked up the call, you know. So let me explain that at LSU, we were inseparable. If we weren't together, we were on the phone together. We went out oh, it got to be that. On Monday and Tuesday, we would rest. So Danny was responsible for looking after me. He always got the job of driving me home. He would take the car, pick me up for school in the morning, and it would start all over again. So there is a recording of Danny Leona conversation, I answer the phone. Danny says a sentence, Then I say, "*Who* is this?" And he laughs and answers as if I really didn't know. So I'm not sure who was fooling who or if it was all fun and games. But we laughed and laughed and laughed. There is also Suzanne. She's got a French-sounding name. We went to high school and LSU.

We had a lot of classes together at LSU. She worked at the paper, and I would go and watch. In college, every Thursday afternoon, Danny, Suzanne, Myrtis (Suzanne's roommate and our messmate), and I would go to this bar called The Chimes. All the waiters knew us and what we would order. Those were the good times. Both Danny and Suzanne live here. It was Suzanne first, then me, and then Danny. Danny was on the extended tour of duty. We never thought he would make it. Was that an intended transition?

What of your best friend? Jealousy and envy appear to be the same. No more pain. Enough agony. Felt that.

What's next? I think, I shall be happy and laugh. I haven't been laughing very much; I've been too busy with my pain.

Bill, Bill, Bill,

Where would I be without you?

Thank you, again and again. Thanks for giving me so much of your time and energy and love. And now, I can't imagine life without you. Thank you for pulling my head out of the clouds and showing me the truth and giving me my life back. What gifts!

So what is the situation with the cold, then? Are you finished?

Lee

Railroad Underpass Photograph with Highway Markers

Sub: Rise and SHINE
Date: 12/12/9910:10:51 AM Eastern Standard lime
From: LEHUFF67
To: NYCblackout

So, Bill,

What if I told you that I did both at once, slept and smiled? I had trouble sleeping. I couldn't stop thinking—thinking, thinking, thinking about you. And smiling.

And the days went by, like paper in the wind, everything changed, then changed again. It's hard to find a friend? It's hard to find a friend. And it changed their lives. And the days went by like paper in the wind. Everything changed then changed again. It's hard to find a friend. It's hard to find a friend.

Yeah. It overlaps, and we bump up against each other. We do keep meeting and understanding and knowing we know. I know you know I know. And back again. And again and again and again. And, and, and, well. There you have it. There you go. There it is.

Oh. Oh. Oh. What can I say? Nothing needs to be said. And they sat quietly in the silence and thought of all the wonderful things they would each do with their lives. I don't know, but I do know. It's not scary so much, as it is overwhelming, and it is magic. Both made magic. Magic. Magic. Magic.

I don't know. Now I am scared. It's too much to take in at once but not to believe in. I believe it. But can't. Ok. Ok ok. OK. Ok. OK!

You know how it is when all along you know it's not really you. I don't know, perhaps you don't buy into it so much subconsciously. So maybe you're only half invested. So it's done. *Finito vamous. Allon.* We go.

We have gone. We went into this, and I didn't realize it until after we got here. I did realize we were going. But *boom*. I've just woke up to it. *Wow*. It just happened.

Did you know we were going? When did you know? You knew before me. It seems I am always the last to find out. Always. But I know why. I am always fooling myself, playing tricks on myself. So silly, I am.

You follow your feelings. You follow your dreams. So what's in there waiting? Neither one of us knows. You might find someone to help you get over the pain that will come, but you're just a poor boy a long way from home. All alone in this world, and it's wake-up time. Time to open up your eyes and rise and shine.

For goodness' sake!

So the time has come. The time has come for all good men. What is that from?

We should set a meeting, have an appointment. Specify a time and place for a face to face, somewhere dark with a personality, like Limerick Junction, not loud but with music and not so many people but enough so that we can have the energy of that. Where is that place? You tell me. Tell me. Tell me.

And indeed there will be time. Time to make a face for the faces you will meet. Time to murder and create time. There will be time. There will be time.

I didn't know about the fever. How much was there? Fever.

Scary that is.

It is not too much, what you say. It's never enough.

Lee

Letting Go

Sub: Re: Rise and SHINE
Date: 12/12/99 11:03:45 AM Eastern Standard Time
From: NYCblackout
To: LEHUFF67

Morning,

I could hardly sleep at all. Every time I turned over—beads of sweat. Out of the darkness, a slither of light. Circling around and over. Forming a halo. Frightened. Afraid. An outstretched arm, connecting your aura. Releasing, hollering in sync, barely with contemplation.

Really this was not the plan. I had no intention for these feelings to be so prevalent. Strong. Tender. Soft. Exotic. All at once. Yet I'm like a little boy just after midnight on Xmas. Anticipating Santa's departure. Wishing for quiet just before opening presents. Waiting and happy. I'm happy, from the thought of your voice. Glad from the look of your eyes as we open up to discovery. Maybe sharing so much more with you. It's scary. It's a good scary.

Your vibe on the phone rubbed a warm spot. We got to be careful. I must not be the one to interfere with your process of healing. You're getting squared away. It would be way below human to form a creature of spirits. Feels just like we're taking big steps. The weight is so light, from what has been peeled away.

When I think about you, I only see you. I don't envision anybody before you or anybody around you. I'm spotting you as free. Free to walk with your head up. I see you moving forward, kicking up some dirt. Turning heads with your charm. Bowling cats over with your writing. Unfolding into such a golden array of essence and spirit, that none will have the balls to challenge. Not that you'll be scaring folks. They'll just see more of your confidence. They'll be attracted to your core. Growing out yonder and beyond a dark cloud. I felt a lot of you. Steady, on my mind.

I happen to miss you. I'm missing a glow from your smile. I can only imagine what it feels like to touch you, without pretenses. Without those earlier fears. There's so much I want to tell you. I'm wishing you a full prosperous day. Hope you have fun with your guests.

I'll submit a small prayer to the Creator.

Peace,

Bill

Red Pane Door with green trees and shrubs photograph

Sub: Re: Rise and SHINE
Date: 12/12/993:08:06 PM Eastern Standard Time
From: LEHUFF67
To: NYCblackout

Bill,

I could think of nothing but you all day. Whenever someone spoke to me, when I looked at anything. When I knew you would have responded to me, I knew you would have answered me. I knew. I knew. I knew.

I think that I am so used to that nothingness. That was good. That I am OK to be. Don't worry about it. There is nothing to worry about. We should just be. What we know and feel to be true and real. You know and I know you know I know.

You have become cautious and quite. I think that is out of respect. Thank you. But let us not waste anything, time. Emotion. Time. Time. Time and tide wait for no man! No man is an island. And we have already been through the shipwreck and the reaching of the shore. Let us be what it is we are to be.

This was not the plan. Who had a plan? Who knew? Neither of us had an inkling. Neither you. Neither me.

An, as you know, therein lies the beauty of it. You asked me if I was that actress everyone was talking about. What was that about? Don't answer this question. I want an answer. Do I embody that?

One Mardi Gras moment before I moved to Atlanta, I was telling of my plans to move, someone turned to me and asked, "So what are you going to be, an actress/model? What?" No. No. No. I'm just going to be whatever I turn out to be. Other people get confused about the physical. So what? So was I created to be this way? I don't have time to think about it now. I must have done it for a reason.

But as you well know, it's not who I am deep inside. It's flash. Maybe I need that to become who I need to be? I'm just intrigued about that whole thing. About what it is that provoked you to say that?

Now it seems I take the lead.

And we shall not be afraid. We shall go and do what needs to be done, for you for me. Or us—whatever that turns out to be.

Monday. Monday. Monday.

Lee

Sub: what is the subject? It seems to rely heavily on both the verb and object.
Date: 12/12/999:39:28 PM Eastern Standard Time
From: LEHUFF67
To: NYCblackout

But you can't start without the subject can you? No. So what is the subject? It should be clear by now. So tell me, who is the man in the moon? Not the moon. The expression.

And how did he get there? What is he doing with his time? How did he get there? What can he possibly be eating?

Oz,
Lee

Bird House Photograph

Sub: This is the way Emerson and Twain Saw It.
Date: 12/14/99 9:09:21 AM Eastern Standard time
From: LEHUFF67
To: NYCblackout

> Our chief want in life is somebody who will make us do what we can. (Ralph Waldo Emerson)
>
> Keep away from people who try to belittle your ambitions. Small people always do that, but the really great make you feel that you too, can become great. (Mark Twain)

So I seek, am seeking, have sought validation. Yes, confirmation. "Yes, Madame, you got it! You can make it happen. You got what it takes. We believe in your ability. We see your potential. We have crossed The Styx River. We have walked through the fire and ice. You can make it. Go get your suit. The rest of it, the true grit, the ability to swim, stir the fire and flames of everlasting hell, and the cold dark night. This should not be your concern. Leap. And the net will appear." It is validation.

I have no desire to emulate anyone. The greatness of the power and majesty of mystical creation of the revelation, the quaking. Have I the essence, the uniqueness, a chance, the foothold? Do you see in me possibility, the potential, to make a mark, to make my mark on the face of the earth, such as that? If the answer be yes, then in my mind, the next step is, I need a map. As you all have. Approached the crossing, walked thru hell, fallen into the pits and crawled out, what scars have you?

What is the medicine, where is the cure, and then, what happens? Is it winter, spring, summer, or fall? Oh, the spring. And do the red bud trees survive it thru a late frost, or must I have two springs before the glory, before the magical mystery tour begins? A map? Can you show me the way, not do it for me, not follow step for step in the footprints of another, not the scary steps, but the road, not the same road. The way.

These things I know. But the things you're never told can tear you apart. And then, he gave her a map. He gave her a map. After all of that, He gave her a map. The first map. Good God. What a rugged road.

And now, I express to you my gratitude, once again. And am again overwhelmed by it, by your generosity. Thank you. What I need, desire, now, at this point in *my life* is get on the road and mow, mow, mow. I can take whatever pain comes along. What I know of pain! I am not afraid to suffer, for many of my days have been spent in the lap of suffering and despair.

I know how to wait for the day to look back. I'm going to be living to tell. There is no doubt about that. It's all about survival. All of it! Oh. And so then, the lesson may very well be—you can't be told by another artist that, "Oh, yeah. You can." You have to pick up the scraps. The bits. The pieces. The tiny particles. Because of jealousy and envy and competition. Because of what you have said. And what I know. It's all in the how of it, keeping it inside—a secret. It's a secret, ah, there it is. Plain as day! It's a secret!

What a fool am I? But no more.

So the other revelation is the 21st Century. My mission. Why they sent me back, again. Wake up call! It's always so simple, isn't it? And the problem is always the same. I'm not paying attention. It's love. Try and figure out love. Jesus Christ! Good God Almighty.

You need to let go of it. And I mean, now! Stop! Cease and desist. That road is closed. But I don't remember opening it, any way! And that is the sticking point, Macbeth! Out damned spot. Out! Now and forever. The end. Amen. Got it? Good.

So now I'll dream my own dreams. Quietly. But you know about Broadway. You saw it before I did. Didn't you? But it was the actress, not the playwright. Again. I didn't see anybody when I was there. I don't know who was there. So I don't know if you will make it or not. But I'll send an invitation. OK? OK.

Va Bene.

Peace,
Lee

Front Porch, Empty Swing Set Photograph

Sub: Re: Consider THIS
Date: 12/14/99 12: 11:40 AM Eastern Standard lime
From: NYCblackout
To: LEHUFF67

You ask me what I think of your art. You suggest somebody I never meet compares your writing to Truman Capote? I don't know where you're coming from? You're pissed off, by my lack of confirmation. So you want to stop writing to me. It's not so complicated. Grab what's happening on the inside, not on the surface. Faulkner. Clancy. James. Irving. Angelo. Capote. Why not you?

You're looking outward, for an answer. Nobody on the outside can help you. Tons of suggestions and rumors, but no answers.

Explore your anger. Is it anger from missing something or wanting something? Does it make you anxious to get to your lap top or back to your desk to jot down an emotion. Check it out—if it's taking root in the deepest cavity of your heart. Do you sense a shuffling of thoughts—an old memory, crazy passions? Does all of this send you reeling, out of control? Then something nags at you, pulling you to frame an image, from a tiny thought.

Through the smoke and haze, you're searching for an invisible morsel of hope. A teeny-weeny step. There'll be a few more and then bigger ones to come. When you start going through wrinkles, your faith is at its darkest shadow. A consolation is that just under and around the darkness, is a ray of light. From there, you might be near madness, but you're moving in another direction. You might be close to anxiety, but it can only slide off your back. After all, you're beginning to see now!

You're free to move closer to nature. Not on a post card. Not on a photograph. Not a museum wall. Rather, an aura you reveled in as a child. Playing alone. Talking to yourself. Giggling from a silly word. Getting excited about your own lines. Embracing you for the first time. Creating a destiny out of nothing.

It appears like you're moving. Traveling, without leaving your spot. A lightness seeps in. A simple stare over to the trees, puts you on a walk in the woods. Nobody around. A slight breeze, bearing serenity. From the corner of your eye, you spot a baby deer, romping under a low hanging tree limb. Nibbling leaves. Maybe the baby deer is taking off for the first time. It could be on the prowl for fragrant leaves. Between nowhere, your eyes meet. You detect a feeling of familiarity, a companionship, a lost friend—from way long ago. Alas—at one spot. A unique specie. A different animal. At this moment, all bets are off. Another rhythm takes over.

Recall a foolish moment. Remember when you were scared. Take a time out from "thinking this and thinking that." Walk around with your emotions. Inexpressible sensations. Fleeting words. A stranger's touch on your shoulder.

It so happens that our secrets are nothing more than an unfinished dream, an unexplained heartbreak, an unforgiven hurt, an incomplete emotion—a slipping mirage. You know this scene better than anybody.

Peace,
Bill

Intentions

Sub: Re: Snap out of it
Date: 12/14/99 11:34:01 PM Eastern Standard lime
From: NYCblackout
To: LEHUFF67

Everything passing in front of the eye is real. Our imagination could bear no fruit. A simple feeling, could lack hope—courage. Wondering, as it fleets over yonder. It is a remnant from yearning. Longing. Lusting. Seeking. Unsettling? Unrelenting as it slips through a crack of the hand.

You're standing in tall cotton. There have been a few folks who have raised hell and lived to talk about it—like Ayn Rand. Eldridge Cleaver. Ernest Hemingway. Toni Morrison. John Paul Sartre. Stephen King. Tennessee Williams. Mother Theresa. John Irving. James Baldwin. Pat Conroy.

It's not that you want to holler up a storm or what not. All you're seeking is to get out there. Travel the road in your own way, as you see the turns. Riding the clutch if you want. Putting the foot to the pedal if you must. A crazy, mixed-up bag. Sporadically accentuated with a beat, exploding an eardrum. Gingerly touching upon an area, undetectable to the eye.

There are tons of folks who identify with your vibes: Weaving rage. Unpredictable context. Quiet passion. Quirkiness.

Reminiscent ancient
Persian Tapestry
Resonant hues
Intricate loops
Simpatico

Suspended animation
Connecting depths
Quaint ensemble
Merging delicate
Tracing detail
Forging succinct
Life kernels
Reflecting vibrancy
Mysterious signals
Harboring lightness

How much time do you want to devote to it? How much energy do you give it? How well do you want to take care of it? How much concern are you going to give to maintain it? Will you actually keep it a secret, until it's ready to blow them out of the water?

Along the way, you'll become good buddies with patience.

At times, you will become very lonely, so lonely you won't even like yourself. What did I do to deserve this action? You'll cry a lot. You'll lose track of what's really happening to you. On occasion, you'll second-guess yourself. Maybe, shoot yourself in the foot! Then you'll gather up yourself up from the floor. Finish off a glass of red wine. Swallow a "mother's helper." You might even go so far as drowning your face in a mug of black coffee. Wake up, Little Suzy!

Part of the magic of what you're doing is so much about the unknown. That is why I beseech you to keep your mouth shut. Keep your destination a secret. Nobody needs to know. They haven't gone there. Down south or over there, near deep forests. You're the one who understands what it takes to get there.

This is your ride. It is your trip. Share it with yourself. Often or rarely, whatever.

Yet don't take yourself too seriously. Remember you're describing an essence, a truth— something urgent.

In coming to the plate, you're humbling yourself to others. Drawing from. Don't need them. Curious—not interested in finding. Really, not caring about what other people say. No roots, much like the baby deer in the forest.

Wandering around aimlessly—you get to sense another side. One becomes familiar with an unknown. Hesitation nudges toward acceptance.

Everything is all right. If folks want to lie to you, it is all right. If somebody wants to rip you off, completely all right too. It's ok, if they want to take advantage of your curiosity. That's cool too. It really doesn't matter. Keep in mind, desperation seeks out strange bedfellows.

Please remember your best friend—patience. Patience is everything, and I can't tell you too much about something—you're in the process of learning. But you'll discover much more than any book could say on the matter. Don't stoop to a level, from which you're leaving. A memory recalls an experience, from which some of the details remain absent.

Don't forget that you're creating. Creating an idea. Developing a story. Embellishing spirit. Actors are no one else, besides a soul striving to live a healthy life. Writers are street savvy observers, aiming to understand something about a feeling they've only imagined up until this point. So each discovery paves an avenue aimlessly to the next point of demarcation, awakening.

An artist (farmer, painter, ditch digger, potterer, musician, dancer, nurse, singer, doctor, preacher, drummer, sculptor, mechanic, chef, actor, mother or writer) listens for a deeper beat - a beginning is the start of an ending or an ending is the start of a beginning.

Time has it's own rhythm. Crawling around and underneath the table, even when you don't see it—is your soul. Simmering with aromas and fragrances from a bunch of Texas Yellow Roses, in late spring. Sometimes you'll find yourself smiling and crying at the same time.

Bill

Old White House Staircase Photograph

Sub: you
Date: 12/15/99 8:21:10 PM Eastern Standard time
From: LEHUFF67
To: NYCblackout

Bill,

Why is the phone busy?

Bill, oh, my God!

Never in my life has someone shown and given to me in such a profound and spiritual way. I cried. Again.

I can't believe you. I can't believe you. I don't know what to say. I don't know how to say it. Oh, my God! You are amazing and wonderful.

Oh, Bill! Thank you. For this and for things I don't, am unable to understand. I don't know what to say. Once again I am overwhelmed. I can't see through the tears, call me.

Lee

Sub: Re: Waiting is the hardest part
Date: 12/16/99 12:00:58 PM Eastern Standard lime
From: LEHUFF67
To: NYCblackout

Bill,

You know, where did you, how did you, how is it possiblc that you can know and say all of that? How do you know all of that? How can you say it the way you do? I can't express it. I've never been here before, and I don't know what to say. I am beyond overwhelmed, and now for you, to you, I need to express more than gratitude. What are those things? Are we to name them?

Is it all about the past? Is it because of the past, we can move like this? Is it because we are aware of the possibilities that we can do and be this? It is because, yes, of the belief, because of what we believe in and of and to be not only possible but probable. Good God Almighty! It's much too much, sometimes, to comprehend, not that I think I do completely.

We have landed.

It must be that we have met more than twice before. I think there was struggle, competition, but now that we had fought the battles of the war, and it is over, it was testing each other, challenging, ancient, no doubt, pagan. We fought for a long time, but we never lost respect for the fight or each other. We are sportsmen, and now that has all fallen away, the fight, and we meet again to work together. *Oh!*

The hardest part and the best part. Yeah. Yeah. Oh, you don't say? Ummmmmm. It's so difficult, so painful, so tragic, to have something to suffer for and over, but then again, what else are you going to do?

La. La. Los Angeles

Observation Dorothy Parker

> If I don't drive around the park, I'm pretty sure to make my mark. If I'm in bed each night by ten, I may get back my looks again. If I abstain from fun and such, I'll probably amount to much. But I shall stay the way I am, because I do not give a hoot. damn.

Dorothy. She had a wit. And a tongue. I go now back to sleep. I can say no more. I must rest.

Lee

Colorful Wall Painting Photograph

Sub:
Date:
From: LEHUFF67
To: NYCblackout

It seems to me that the minute, the second I catch my breath and can feel firmly planted on the ground, there is yet another occasion to arise to and fro.

I can't keep up, I don't have time to think, and you know I need time to think! I don't have time enough to read and reread all that you send. I'm not complaining. I'm making a statement of my position—my feelings.

I cannot tell you. I don't even know what I am trying to say. But perhaps, maybe, even, the thing of it is—I don't have to.

Lee

Sub: Re: Bon.jomo
Date: 12/17/99 11:02:43 AM Eastern Standard lime
From: LEHUFF67
To: NYCblackout

My sleep was not so fantastic. It was fitful. I awoke, at each thought, seeking to understand, wanting to get it and move beyond, move forward, up and over, and into.

I understand about my characters being me, what I know and understand to be true and real and actual and mine. I got that last night. Just needed time to think about it. Time and quiet spaces. Places. So now I must do the work. Oh, it's so difficult. Why am I afraid of creation? Self-doubt? Fear of success? Why? I know, I'll just do it.

I know you're out there, in the bubble we created. I feel high above and beyond, and I think we should leave this place. It's too much for me, the everyday noise and interference and ugliness and all that red and yellow plastic. Lighting up the road to nowhere. I want to see only trees and birds and mountains and the ocean and the clouds in the sky and the stars at night and the moon and the sun (shining everyday) and quiet and peace and quiet. And simple, everything simple and easy to manage and deal with. Simple, simple, simple.

We said we would talk about if I go or if we go. Either way, we are together. I think perhaps I need time to do what is before me. Time to sit and think and figure. I need this for me. I don't want to regret not doing it, and I know you don't want that for me either. So we will talk and plan and then move and go and do and be and become. Who we are, as individuals and as us.

I am thinking of tobacco.

So, good Lord, can we rest a minute? I have complete system overload. Can we get off the rocket for a minute, maybe visit Mars or Jupiter, have lunch, look around, and take a walk? It's like finals.

Lee

Running to You

Sub: a beginning…means a departure
Date: 12/19/99 11:59:59 AM Eastern Standard time
From: NYCblackout
To: LEHUFF67

Leaving something behind just means you're going to another place. It's not necessary to condemn the stuff you leave behind. You're just heading some place others haven't been. So you think. You're heading over to the other side. That place you were always afraid to explore. That dark spot which was forbidden. The off-limits area. It's a scene where everything you used to dream about, is happening all around you. Momma's got a brand-new bag! A brand-new memory.

Wish them well. Avoid the conditional. "I'll come back for you. I'll tell you all about it when I get there. I'll send you a telegram." We've heard it before. You've reached it all by your own reserves: your wit, your power, your guts—not from the folks, you left behind.

A seed, under earth
An embryo unfolds
Seeking space
Surrounding nutrients
Compost, fertilizer
Water, oxygen aplenty

All that matters, is the one who grows.

Bill

Wall Vine Growing Photograph

Sub: Re: a beginning…means a departure…
Date: 12/20/99 12:23:22 PM Eastern Standard lime
From: LEHUFF67
To: NYCblackout

Look and Listen:

1. No one is to ever impose upon me a thing. I am my own person. I shall and do make my own choices and decisions. I will not be instructed on how to think and feel and act. You almost had your hooks in me, had me bound and tied. No. No. No. I am not about being told, controlled. Not at all.
2. As much as you want it to be, this will never be romantic love (*Eros*). I don't want that from you. Get it? Got it? Good. Forget about it. Never will it be that the physical realm is entered into. Never. Do I have to say it again? How many more times? You know what? I will never say it again. If you place me in that arena again, it's lights out. The show will be over, the curtain drawn, down to the floor, and there will be no encore. None.

Excuse me, but what about the energy I put into the above #2? Ok. How do you see that impacting my art? There you go. Don't mess with me. Don't play mind games with me. You'll never get over on me.

It has been said by those much older and wiser than I, that I am nobody's fool.

How arrogant of you to assume and presume to know a thing about my relationships. Were you there?

Did you experience my life? Have you felt what I felt in the moment I felt it? And do you know the Hell l have walked through? And did you see who held my hand and carried me out? No. You had no concept of what I have done and been and seen and who was there, and how they loved me. This love, the love I share with Daniel, my brother, my wry brother, is not for you to question, disregard, and attempt to cast away. Danny is and was and will be always the first person to have loved me outside of my family. The road of Leona and Daniel is long and winding and joyous and wicked and beautiful and delightful and wonderful and sacred to me and him. How dare you. You can think and see whatever you want. I don't care.

You simply have no concept. None whatsoever. I don't have time for this or that. I am telling you for the last time all of these things. I'll do whatever I want to do. I have everything I need. I ask for nothing from no one. And in that lies the power. I can do and get and think and be all alone. I don't need permission. I don't need. I got it. From top to bottom, beginning to end, I can stay or I can go either way. It's my decision. I can get there alone. I can go anywhere I choose. The moment I choose and no one. No one is in my way. So get out of my way, because you put yourself there, again. And that's it. The end. Amen.

We go to this place again?

Sub: The 2nd GREAT Summing UP
Date: 12/22/99 5:30:40 AM Eastern Standard time
From: LEHUFF67
To: NYCblackout

Yep. So I'm awake. I believe you had something to do with that, so let's talk. Shall we?

Respect. Respect. I would think, would fathom, would hazard a guess that you, professor of dolling it out, would/should be able to read the lines, which I will leave unwritten on this subject. Thank you.

What have I been saying all along about being a woman? Do you need a recap? Good. I'm wanting nothing more than to become what I can and what I desire to become outside of the mere fact that I am female. This fact does not define, completely and totally who I am as a human being. Enough.

This is what I want.
This is what I need.
This is what I loved.
The association.
The working.

Sub: Re: The 2nd GREAT Summing UP…
Date: 12/22/999:05:29 AM Eastern Standard Time
From: NYCblackout
To: LEHUFF67

You say get lost. I'm feeling, we found something. Why do they have to be two different notions? If you were a mocking bird, hopping from your nest, over to a high limb on an old oak tree, why can't I observe the flight?

Your ship has just left port on the way to a sweet spot. Yet your trip has nothing to do with anything. No connection to time. No woman's rights. No southern heritage. Has anybody gone before you? What is the name of the soul who owns time?

As you navigate to a higher plateau, your hopes and dreams come, not directly at you, but from an angle, slanted with the things that once were quite familiar. Before now, there were lots of opinions, suggestions disclosures, data, criticisms, doubts, and revelations. Oftentimes, the rumors follow you from one spot and arrive before you land. You could go around thinking that if you make a right move, everything could be just behind you.

Changing and a willingness to change is what we're shouting about on the phone. It's the reason we holler and roll eyes. The backbone of my tears, late at night is this shifting, under my feet. A slow feeling comes over and confirms that the angle is not so strange. The hill, not so high. The moon, not too far away. Our love, our hopes, all within a thumb's nail.

You're creating a chance to hook up with different unique craftspeople. They'll be inspired by your diligence. They'll admire your attention to detail. Your work will be a source of wonder, as you wander along your path toward destiny.

Hoping that peace abides with you, your family, and other folks you love.

Bill

Sub: Revelations
Date: 12/25/99 1:09: 10 PM Eastern Standard Time
From: rudy.hall@att.net
To: LEHUFF67@AOL.COM
CC: NYCBLACKOUT@AOL. COM

So many thoughts. So many horizons. Sensing a vast plateau. New images connect with ancient meditations. A fresh sensation gets acquainted with an old impulse.

Right now, my thoughts and sweat are on top of *Le Edison Effect*. Crystallizing. Integral fabric. Touching. Imploring discovery. Hearing from bases out of sight being directed, sauntering, guided by an invisible offensive.

I've been really thinking about you. Hoping your holiday unfolds prosperity. Bounty. Happiness.

Not only,
During this moment
Way beyond juncture
Your future

Kindness,
Bill

Sub: Missing u
Date: 12/27/99 3:22:19 AM Eastern Standard Time
From: NYCblackout
To: LEHUFF67

Hola

I've been missing you. The sound of your voice. Our connection. Our empathy. Our spot. Suspended. Hopelessly.

Yet it's been a quiet separation. All our wishes have been directed toward your goals. Objectives. Dreams. Desires. Hopes. I'm unable, to think beyond your thoughts, discoveries, unraveling.

I happen to love you. Yes, I have love for you. Tiny. Wide. Deep. High. I hope your flower continues to unfold, brightly.

Wishing you well,
Bill

Sub: arriving
Date: 01/08/00 1:47:07 PM Eastern Standard Time
From: NYCblackout
To: LEHUFF67

Sounds like you're arriving at a juncture. A crossing point. Do you sense a new energy? Is it a happy notion to actually touch what you've felt all during the journey? No longer a wretch; no wandering around. Now I can see glory cascading on the horizon. Running through and thorough. No time to check out the scars. Later for that old time jive. Off with the hassle. Time to acknowledge. Time to embrace your own steps.

You've traveled a long road, on the way. Just a few more miles to go until you discover a layer of essence. Until you uncover spectacular. Dwelling quietly between spirit and mind, as mother wisdom reveals clarity. Until your love elevates upward, outward & beyond.

I'm really happy for you.

Peace,
Bill

Green Shrub Photograph

Sub: (no subject)
Date: 01/10/00 10:31:13 PM Eastern Standard Time
From: NYCblackout
To: LEHUFF67

Hey,

Stick to your story! Follow your gut. Keep up your insight on getting details worked out. Italy, travel, knowing the other side of strangers and unveiling a kink or two in your armor.

Please, if you will allow me, stay close to your character. Move aside, as they tell you about your story. Embolden them with your courage. Share your instincts with them. Show them your soft spots. Don't be afraid to let them overpower you. Don't be afraid to let them know that you're afraid. You could take side trips with them. It would be really cool to get lost with them, drink a six-pack. These folks are not so far from you. You might want to drift along with them, into an unknown, unfamiliar area. You might end up near a comfort spot, where it comes down to understanding.

A sensation. Echo. Reflections as they stretch out over a space larger than the Grand Canyon. Not only is your head pointing to the clouds while your feet kick up dirt. No longer anything to hide from. It's due primarily to your arrival with awareness. Everything is under the same spot. Over there, where time is nothing but an impulse.

Good and good thoughts are what I'm hoping for you, your family, your friends, and any souls who have wandered along your path—on the way to over yonder.

Loving you feels like magic.

Bill

Circling Back

Sub: another time
Date: 01/11/00 11:20:39 PM Eastern Standard Time
From: NYCblackout
To: LEHUFF67

It's a feeling of getting there. An awakening. Something is agitating the soul, without notice. An unforeseen energy cycles near by. Your very first instinct is to fight it off. A denial. It's too good to be true. It's not what we anticipated. It could be too heavy to bear. All of this creates a sense of loss and wondering.

Yet we want to know, where it is all of this coming from. We want to know more about it. What manner of power is this, that awakes one from deep slumber, that swerves conflicting waves away from shore, that swells an anxious heart, which leans away while lingering ever so closely? A question comes to bear on why was I chosen. Is this a core of life? Could be this be enlightenment?

It's an existence that wasn't on the map before we met. You've been close by all the time, and now, I'm seeing an image that was beyond possible. When I'm bad, you've already forgiven me. When I'm good, it was what you anticipated. When I'm afraid, you extend an uplifting word. When I wallow in doubt, you're just around the corner, offering a connection. I feel a lot for you. I'm feeling you, all around me.

Drive careful on the way back to Florida. Watch the road. Keep working on Italy. You'll be there before you know it. It's only another leg of the journey. Drifting. Near destiny. I'm with you. There's much power between us. Around what we're hoping for. Working on. Near awesome, some kind of magnitude. Escaping boundaries.

Being near you is similar to floating in a circle. Surrounded by a circumference of your arms.

I'm missing a tone. A particular ringing from your voice. Just as you move from a corner of your heart. Entering my soul. Carrying a thunder's roar.

Until the future, not so far away.

Bill

Sub: another time
Date: 01/12/00
From: LEHUFF67
To: NYCblackout

Thank you.

I can't say any more. I can't. I can't imagine what, how, it would be.

HowI would stay on my path. This path. Without your support and love.

I think I would have fallen back into the pit. The bottoms.

Thank you for believing in me and my dreams.

You'll never know.

Lee

Sub: Sunday-poetry reading @Sacred Ground
Date: 01/28/00 12:26:26 AM Eastern Standard Time
From: NYCblackout
To: LEHUFF67

Hey,

Sunday night, would you like to go to a poetry reading @ Sacred Ground? 510 Flat Shoals. East Atlanta Village. It's a bakery. Coffee bar. Tea place. T-shirts and antiques hang out. If you feel like you want to read, go for it. The show sounds like care free and going for the jugular. If you have plans, I'll understand.

Momentarily
Dark world
Cruel
Intruding
Missing
Dreams
Rescue you
Let downs
Deceptions
Love game
Power deal
Substitute feelings
Simple gratitude
Kind gesture
Honeysuckle wind
Flutterby flight
Beautiful loom
Connecting spirits
Destinations
Tangled thoughts
Glee

Bliss
Flowery blossom
Gone inhibition

Until I hear from you, you have my hopes that peace continues to be abide with you, wherever you go.

Bill

Sub: (no subject)
Date: 01/28/00 12:18:40 AM Eastern Standard Time
From: LEHUFF67
To: NYCblackout

What are you doing?

Lee

Sub: Questions
Date: 1/28/00 9:12:02 PM Eastern Standard Time
From: LEHUFF67
To: NYCblackout

Why this sadness? Why all this rubbish figuring it out, finding out about. There is no avoiding it. There is no way to not examine what happens.

I long for the end. I think I have covered every possible arena, person, place, and thing. I think I have cleaned and cleared most every possible thing. The doctors, the mother, the father. The cousins and the friends and now, in my hand, I hold a very few, so very few.

But now I know
Who is true and real?
Who I can call
Who can help?
Who will want to help?
Who will be there for the long haul?

And for this I am most grateful. For this, I can choose more wisely and safely. It is hard to face. It is difficult; it hurts. It's like waking up to a whole new world. It's like being a baby all over again. Trying to find the way. The answers. The words. The meaning.

It makes me sad
I have gone inside
I have gone inside
I must be careful
I must remember who I am and what I want and how to.
I have missed you

Help me get out of here, out of this.
I doubt myself
I doubt my ability
I am so scared.

Lee

Sub: getting back
Date: 1/29/00 10:06:06 AM Eastern Standard Time
From: LEHUFF67
To: NYCblackout

I feel much stronger. I am back on track, on the block. The key lies deep in another world. Another existence. A world beyond sight.

It is a mystery spot. Holding a raging storm.That rattles the foundation. A foothold into the future to only a few who share know.

The belief
That anything is possible
That whatever it is
Whatever it can be
Whatever can be?
Must not be lost
What I would do
How I would keep my beliefs
In focus, clean,
In check
Without your
Without you, I dare say,
I dare think
What would I do without?
Your belief in me?
You are such a gift
It would be a barren desert
I would be so very alone

Thank God for you.

Lee

Sub: BEING OVER THERE
Date: 01/29/00 10:57:36 PM Eastern Standard Time
From: NYCblackout
To: LEHUFF67

When we escape, there is a real possibility of leaving the past behind. An old memory that refused to go away. An excitement pops up as you throw our line over the horizon. What was old, is new. We feel we're on the way. Our footsteps that were once shaky are now as steady as you go. Quickly, the horror of not knowing disappears.

Slowly, we begin to open up to who we really are—who we were destined to be. We pull out those jewels that were buried in doubt. We step up our game. Feelings are different. Knowing you are in my life makes a huge difference. You are to be commended for your bravery. I've learned more about my own bravery, by seeing you in action.

Since you been coming around,
I'm aware of something different
A fuller, deeper understanding of love
A solid feeling – once off the map
Creeping where
No mindful being, would expect
Similar to an old gas lantern
Dangling around a cold dark room
Revealing a warm vibration
Old memories
Appear lighter
Foreign evolves to domestic
Hassle no more
Soft feelings emerge
Still waters calm

The more, I know about you
The more, I want to know about you

Until I hear more,

Bill

Bird Pool, with leaves Photograph

Sub: Re: BEING OVER THERE...
Date: 01/29/00 11:49: 17 PM Eastern Standard Time
From: LEHUFF67
To: NYCblackout

You say the most beautiful things to me.

Storybook things.

Thank you for being there in my life for seeing me. For valuing me. For knowing and wanting to know me.

Lee

Sub: March
Date: 02/11./00 1:23:17 AM Eastern Standard lime
From: LEHUFFF67
To: NYCblackout

Aquarius

Prepare for a life-changing decision. You know where fulfillment is to be found. The struggle is in getting there. Don't follow what someone else thinks is best.

You must be a rebel and live by your own rules for happiness. Professionally, a lucky door will open.

Your reputation is on the line and you have to assume responsibility. You have the freedom to imprint your ideas on others.

LUCKY DAYS: Money & Career: March 8 Your golden day: March 2

So what do you think about that? Sorry to have missed your calls. Will be gone all day Saturday. Call around 10 PM. I hope you are enjoying your visit. I have missed you.

Lee

Sub: ESSENTIALLY
Date: O2/14/00 11:00:45 PM Eastern Standard Time
From: NYCblackout
To: LEHUFF67

You're on my mind
At every turn of the road
As each step impresses
Thoughts of you
Run ever deeply
During a lonely time
Solitaire
Independently
They dwell upon a path
Of contemplation
Over to unconsciousness
Where one usually forgets everything

Often my sleep is layered by dreams of life with you. A crazy warm feeling of being next to you. Erupting wildly. Passionately. Sparks explode when your energy hovers like a late-night fog.

I imagine a gentle touch
Tracing, fingers
Lifting a veil from your face
Nervously observing
Certain calm
A bold look
A quiet beauty
Is it possible to love somebody?
So deep, knowing zero about their predecessors
Quietly embracing idiosyncrasies; wrinkles; moles; warts; odd eyes
Every dark spot

Is love a protracted trip, over desolate terrain?
Not an overnight sensation
An ally of time
Patience
Diligence
Consideration
Sharing
Wills
Symbiosis
Metamorphosis

Unannounced, something new appears. Fresh perceptions. Flowing energy pops up. Optimism abound. Once doom was a hovering around. A soul is yanked from nowhere. A spirit sheds light on the whole matter. Gradually, inklings create a confirmation.

I hope peace is vigilant with you, your family, your friends, and other folks you love. I have much love for you. Your essence, your spirit runs abound over here.

Peace,
Bill

Sub: Re: Essentially
Date: 02/15/00 12:47:19 PM Eastern Standard Time
From: LEHUFF67
To: NYCblackout

What can I say?

What can I possible say to you?

I find it impossible to comprehend, to fully and completely grasp the entirety of your love.

How did it happen?

I cannot perhaps

I cannot accept it

Perhaps

I am overwhelmed, which would certainly not be out of the ordinary.

It is difficult to imagine.

That is, life without you.

Lee

Sub: The Birthday
Date: 02/16/0000 9:22:20 PM Eastern Standard Time
From: LEHUFF67
To: NYCblackout

I feel terrible to have not been aware that today is your birthday. Awful.

Please forgive me.

And forgive me,

So when? Thursday or Friday? Let's stay in.

Lee

Sub: Waiting
Date: 2/22/00 9:35:28 PM Eastern Standard lime
From: NYCblackout
To: LEHUFF67

And while this is going on, faith is cooking up a storm. Hope sheds nutrients, thru a lonely time. Unsettling moment or two. Confidence drops off strength to hold a walk steady.

Whenever I grow uncertain or is it old man fear coming around? All it takes is a constant on you. Your aura. Your words. Your touch—directing me over to a spot, where I know only you. Unaware of anybody's glimpse of me whispering, just below your ear.

Sauntering near our presence. Passion flies over. A bunch, no not a bunch of collards. A bunch is how I think of you, how I imagine you and how I see you.

Looming in my heart's remote cavity is a rumble. A faint wish. A distant hope that I'll meet you over yonder. Where 2 is 1 and 1 is 2.

Bill

Sub: Re: Waiting
Date: 2/23/00 12: 11: 39 AM Eastern Standard Time
From: LEHUFF67
To: NYCblackout

And now, you know. Perhaps you needed this time, this 6 weeks, for other things. Clearly, you were not ready. The time was not right; you needed to do something else.

Of course, the secret, as you know, is to believe.

You know you did it. You know it's good. That's the hardest part. The rest is a different animal altogether. But you have to learn it for yourself; you have to feel it, see it, and know it. No one can tell you about it, not even your best friend. You won't even listen to your best friend!

There's no time left to lose. Figure out want you want, and create it. Magic creates a future. Yes, it is good to know how to be patient. But the time has come to make a move, leave the BS alone. Figure out how to make it happen, and all the while you are and will be making it happen. Who you are now, is who you are becoming future, present, and past. This is how life happens. Who you are now, is who you are becoming.

Sorry, no more waiting.
It's time to move
So, get off your butt
And get this movie made
I, for one am tired of waiting.
No more waiting.
We are now moving, moving
Move it!

After today,
You are getting closer.
You are moving.
Don't stop!

Lee

Sub: ESCALATING MELLOWING
Date: 02/24/00 11:50:08 AM Eastern Standard Time
From: NYCblackout
To: LEHUFF67

Our love follows a unique path. Tenderly, we walk where it leads us. Each level of existence, another mood swing.

As you learn, I learn. As I understand, it is your understanding. It goes beyond ever. I can't imagine. Living, not knowing you're all right. I don't want to be that far from you, anymore.

Also, I'm grasping part of our meaning from last night. Fright is going away. An uptight feel is fading. Doubts are evaporating. Moving in is a big well of hope. Renewed confidence. Circling around is calm.

I'm reaching out to you, but I find myself with you, already. It's right next to you where I find love. Where at ease takes over, sliding lightly in the palm of our hands.

Where all we want, waits.

Until. Peace.

Bill

Sub: LOVING LOVING YOUR LOVE
Date: 03/01/00 12:04:23 PM Ea5tern Standard lime
From: NYCblackout
To: LEHUFF67

I'm really struggling. I'm looking for a way. I'm searching for a phrase. It could be a word or two describing a different kind of feeling—an entity, transcending time. A feeling that covers a wide area of my soul. Whenever I touch you. Whenever you're on the horizon.

No description comes close to this sensation. A fresh scent of sharing. That quaint touch of yours, your fingers sliding over my heart. Imprinting a warm image near a sensitive artery. Then there's a quiet urge, cascading along with a steady, slow stream of tears.

Some tiny sparkles. Gradually watching. Guiding every footstep, along a silent trail. Angling where hearts dwell. Spirits connect. Enlightenment. Oneness.

Until I hear from you, my wish for you is that peace walks in front, alongside, above you, behind you, and remains your best friend.

Bill

Pulling Up Roots

Sub: Parting
Date: 03/02/00 10:34:06 AM Eastern Standard Time
From: NYCblackout
To: LEHUFF67

It's about that time. Or is it? Is it what we thought? Is it a moment unto itself? What does one make of an unthinkable sensation?

What about a feeling without borders? No time? No structure? Listening to Mango's "Mondi Sommersi" reminds me of what we do…what we talk about. I'm going to work on a writing project this afternoon. Probably won't be here as you're at the airport. Leaving. Parting.

Yet I won't be far away from you. I'm united, bonded, and blended with your energy. It lingers. I do love you, so much. It hurts. But it's a good hurt. The kind of hurt that harbors, hopes, dreams, a vision. My prayer goes across the Big Pond with you.

And I'm hoping that our Master grants all that you wish and that your discoveries bear fruit. Meditating that our Creator removes any obstacle, preventing your growth. Extracts old walls that hold up your arrival over where your spirit and heart embrace. A silent explosion. Where instead of destruction. You pick up on evolvement as your story take on new life.

A warm spot where you'll be feeling happy. Peace. Ciao.

Bill

Sub: Awaiting & 111 + Waiting.
Date: 03/02/00 9:56:49 PM Eastern Standard Time
From: NYCblackout
To: LEHUFF67

I waited a little while, after I got back from the aero port. Really, waiting and hoping that time would take care of a rush of emotions. That went thru my mind @ the aero port. So much went thru my heart, foggy, unclear, and definitely unsettling. That after all, everything will be all right. A glimmer. Stemming from your gold hair band, showing a ray of hope.

Praying and meditating for your landing to be safe. That your friends are taking good care of you. That your cottage is comfortable. That you're rested up from jet lag. That you're finding things well. You're smiling.

I'm working on getting used to the notion of you not being around. But you could be just around the corner. Your head could be resting on my shoulder. Right now, I'm missing your voice. Your utterance. Your pause. Quiet interludes. Beaucoup moments, as your silence radiate glows.

I'm numb. Stillness suspended above a quaint thought—your aura touching me. Good to see you before you flew out.

I was beside myself. Couldn't hold back the tears in the truck, on the way to see you. Just wanted to surprise you. Yet I knew you knew somewhere that I'd be exactly where you saw me.

Hope *peace* is visiting with you, staying longer, allowing patience for you, Mom & Dad, Maggie, Big Momma, cousins, aunts, uncles, nephews, and nieces. Until I hear from you, you have my warmth.

Bill

Sub: Aero port
Date: 3/03/00 8:20: 34 AM Eastern Standard Time
From: NYCblackout
To: LEHUFF67

What's up with a handshake at the aero port? Was it a society thing? A fear of what other folks are thinking? Are you afraid to claim our friendship, regardless of who may be around or what people are thinking? Are you free now?

Was our love a temporary fling? Do you believe it? Is it real to you? Does it ring true? If so, then why does what other folks think really matter? Was it a source of embarrassment to get on an airplane? I felt less than accepted. After hugging a friend good-bye? I felt like a part of you wanted something to move forward. Another part of you, didn't want to let go.

It was a mixed signal. Really hope that the accommodations, people, and circumstances are there for you that you're settling in. Think these first few days are interesting. Adjusting. Reconsidering the situation and working on projects that make up the time.

Yet. Nothing I do can replace our time. As you can tell, there's a void on the table. The way we'd go back & forth, silly laughter and affirmations. Acknowledgements. A minute is an hour, when we're talking. Deep details between verbs, those times on the telephone. Your impromptu arrivals at my job. Then there are those signals to me that everything is all right. Those junctures of existence when I look in your eyes and see your heart. Down deep, I'm sensing that all will be well. Your imaginations—comfortable, near your heart.

Bill

Sub: Considering
Date: 03/03/00 11: 55: 39 AM Eastern Standard Time
From: NYCblackout
To: LEHUFF67

Like you've been only gone for 18 hours or so. It's beyond scope that I miss you this much. See, I walk by places in my apartment where you sat or leaned against the counter or watched me. I'm remembering how you blew out those cigar circles and how some of them came back near your lips. When I look at your dried flowers, the scent fully reminds me of how you felt in my arms, how you looked away and looked back so suddenly. I can't forget the look in your eyes on Friday night when we shared under the candle light.

I just got back from Publix. A thought that you rode with me on that night time mission (when we got the munchies for chocolate) to buy ice cream and coffee. Next thing I knew, I found myself walking down the same aisle we were on. Then, I looked all around, checking the aisle for you. In a silly moment, I found myself waiting for you to pull Dutch chocolate ice cream from of the cooler. I hollered out.

I'm sad that you're not here. But I'm happy to know you're where you want to be among open spaces. Tall trees, rolling hills, unique buildings soft Mediterranean air and native people.

A patina. Embellishing spirit, mind, body, and soul. Praying and hoping that peace abides with you, your new friends, your family, and your dreams.

Ciao.

Bill

Sub: Ummmmmm
Date: 03/04/00 08:41:44 AM Eastern Standard Time
From: NYCblackout
To: LEHUFF67

Really.

I had no real concept of love, until I bumped into you. I didn't know about a feeling before your flame got a hold of me. Your flame resonates, all over the place. Your ember runs from the tip of my toe, to the back of my ear.

I'm imagining crazy things. If you're all right. If you're eating the right food. If you're sleeping like a lamb or a lion. I really want to touch the spot, where you stood and understand what I don't see.

Only a small word, ringing gentle as my heart grows calm. Until I hear from you, my prayer is that *peace* along side, as you make your move in life.

Bill

Sub: Thinking…Hoping…Wishing. On your behalf.
Date: 3/4/009:06:38 PM Eastern Standard Time
From: NYCblackout
To: LEHUFF67

I want to continue where we left off. I want to build on a growing, widening foundation. I want to learn what I need to do—to learn more about a person I'm admiring from a distance. I'm interested in developing an understanding about what is essential to evolvement through love, patience, consideration, unique openings, a big heart, a deep soul, and a broad spirit.

It's about 9:01 PM on Saturday night, and I'm longing for you. I want to be in the same space with you. Isolation hangs around. Yet I'm comforted by thoughts about your courage, stamina. That kick in the butt approach. High above the fray, is your love. It's a solid feeling. There's much underneath, encircling a core.

This is a good time for both of us. Lots of movement on "Sugar & Spice". I can send it's no longer a baby. It's maturing on its own. I've chiseled, and I'm chiseling away the BS. It's a process of opening up. I'm grateful to our Creator. I'm so happy, even as small tears slide down my cheeks.

Still, I miss you. I'm thinking about you, more than I can say. So much during the day and even into the dark of night, as I'm awakened by your touch. You have to know by now that I'm turned on by your charm. Your take on kindness. And if you didn't know it, only your voice can dig deeply, comforting a forgotten corner of an old soul.

However, I don't want to disturb your thing, your space, your timing or rhythm. I don't want to load you down with events and circumstances that could hold you up. Please let me know if I cross that border.

There's a special delicacy floating around. You don't have to be in the next county to receive my respect. You don't have to call me, to honor yourself. You don't have to e-mail, in order to be the sole object of my attention. Our connection is varied, mellow, broad and deeper as time evolves. It expands to a point where I'm touched by you, even though geography separates us. Still I feel nearer to your spot. No one understands me like you do.

Until l hear from you, you have my love

Bill

Green Foilage

Sub: Missing U
Date: 3/5/009:03:34 AM Eastern Standard Time
From: NYCblackout
To: LEHUFF67

I missed your telephone call yesterday. I was @ work. I'm going in now. I'll play hooky this afternoon. I'm off tomorrow. Got a luncheon on Monday with a movie distributor.

Like, I'm missing you a lot. It is strange not to hear you talk, not to feel your energy as you walk around me. Really, it's an empty feeling to check out walls where you stood. I'm respecting our space, our spot, how your hand feels on top on mine.

Until I hear from you.

Peace,
Bill

A Certain Longing

Sub: Getting there
Date: 03/06/00 3:29:47 AM Eastern Standard Time
From: NYCblackout
To: LEHUFF67

Like it's Sunday night/Monday, I just ate the last of the enchiladas we had on Wednesday. What's up with that? I wanted them to last until you got back. Or was it about savoring a thought?

I feel you're out to sea roaming, searching and exploring unmentionable destination. You're embarking on new territory, examining new territory. Seeking a different adventure. Gravitating distant mirages, meeting up with circumstance, while detecting an espresso aroma from just around the corner.

Unaware, a quiet breeze parts thru your hair, alerting you about a mirage. Alluding that a port awaits you. If you drift a certain direction, if you care not to be away for a long time, if you want to call on at anytime, it will be there. Waiting for you to land and drop anchor. Embrace and rest upon a weary shoulder.

One time at a Tom Petty concert, I heard, "Waiting is the hardest part."

If waiting represents an image of silence, quietly seeking patience for a sound, a vibration, a rumble indicating that something else is going on besides, some object standing in front of you, then I've been waiting for you.

Until I detect your vibes, may *peace* continue to visit with you, your family, your new friends. & acquaintances.

Bill

Sub: Sensing
Date: 3/06/00 5:10:52 AM Eastern Standard Time
From: NYCblackout
To: LEHUFF67

I'm sensing your signal all morning long. Wherever I walk around the apartment, I can feel your presence—an essence from your eyes. I can smell you too. Wherever I look, I see you—the way you check me out, that look in your eyes. Even though you're on the other side of the ocean, I'm picking up a glimpse of your other side with me, right now.

> Way over there and here, in the palm of my hand,
> A familiar ring
> A pulsation
> All around me.

Your love runs through and through, then out to space, landing on a peculiar spot. We're following baby seagulls. Flying out and over old raggedy sails above deep waters. Forming a union with dark skies. Imparting light on a forsaken dream.

All the best to you, your family, and the ones you love. Until I sense more of you.

Peace.

Bill

Sub: In Sync
Date: 03/06/00 9:46:53 AM Eastern Standard Time
From: NYCblackout
To: LEHUFF67

As I was e-mailing you (5:10 AM, Monday, 3/06/00), you were on the phone trying to call me. I was considering how much I miss your touch. How much we're on the same spot. Your love looms big over my being. Not even a word or phrase leaves my heart, without your fingerprint.

I'm quite comfortable with your feelings, wishes, and dreams. I'm really hoping that anything you want comes true. I'm still wondering about your love. I'm wondering how the Creator put us in each other's lives.

I love you. Until l hear from you, you have my.

Peace.

Bill

Sub: Writing
Date: 03/06/00 7:09:38 PM Eastern Standard Time
From: NYCblackout
To: LEHUFF67

The meeting with the distributor's agent was cool. I felt good about our process—this deal of sharing a secret to a stranger.

When I think about you, I want to jot down my thoughts and feelings. Is that weird? I'm so used to calling you straight away. But now, I write to you. Surprisingly, I'm struggling through isolation, solitude, and the darkness of being alone. I just can't get used to being away from you.

Each day I'm getting familiar with what's going on. Me here. You over there. Maybe tomorrow I'll learn more about what patience can do to help a lonely man. So I went to Starbucks, and I kept looking at these couples. Some were holding hands. Some of them were simply walking, passing time. I thought about you. Those coffee times, when we were at Intermezzo. Our small chats, sipping espresso. Our back and forth, over a tiny thought. Those tiny moments have unfolded into a huge scene, with you so far away.

So I hope your days are full of prospects (prospecting for gold). I'm wishing that your nights are replete with all that you wish for. Anything you want could be just around the corner from you or within grasp of your hands, or in the depths of your mind. They're waiting to come out, inspired by an impulse.

If you didn't know already, I'm mad about you. And I'm yearning to be with you soon. Vienna, Paris, or Firenze. Somewhere, almost anywhere over there. Until I hear more from you.

Peace.

Bill

Sub: Echonnnnn
Date: 03/07/00 9:26:29 PM Eastern Standard Time
From: NYCblackout
To: LEHUFF67

It's a silent moment. It's something way beyond understanding. Then it's all familiar. Something we've all heard about before. It's a rumor about how one would feel if a certain kind of thing went down. It could've been a comedy on TV. Something on Channel 2 Action News. Somewhere in an old family closet. The very thing nobody wanted to happen. All of a sudden, it happens.

Being isolated and not knowing what to do. At this moment, I'm lonely for you. I'm missing that little spark in your eyes. Your stare into my eyes, making a straight line to my heart. I'm trembling when I think about your walk. The crazy things you say, when you walk around me. Getting from morning to night is rugged. Even with those surges, rhythms, movements, juggles, and flames. My soul rolled over, when your fingers landed softly in the palm of my hand.

Every day I'm learning something else that allows me to take care of it. Yet I haven't been perfect. At times, I lose confidence when that deal happened near around my birthday (a beautiful blond, with eyes you'd kill for). It was a weak lapse of memory. Forgetting how much I wanted you near me. How much I valued our friendship. How much I cherished our love. How I just want to work harder.

So now I'm waiting alone. Waiting without telephone calls. Without human interruptions. Without myself. Feeling sufficient due to our foundation. Our communications. Our empathy. Our distant hopes. Our faith and dreams.

Tonight, I felt a connection to our story. The one I want to write with you. Like we can extract the ambiance of San Francisco and that whole knowledge thing, but we'll play with it. Have some fun like the Greeks. Or like Botticelli with halo, angels.

Anyways, our character is a writer. Success has avoided him like Jungle Fever. He lives in the shadow of other artists. A freelance magazine repair artist. He dabbles in research and stories nobody wants to write about. You could call him a rescue writer—the dude, studios call to "make changes." He's got a reputation of replacing writers who go on vacation. He's a stand-in for life, so to speak. Somebody the industry always call for a particular edge to a story. Somebody who's dispensable as the words he spits from the latest "Final Draft" script.

One day, he gets an e-mail requesting his skills on a huge writing project. But the kicker is that he won't get any print credit for the story. It's for the daughter of a filthy rich industrial magnate with friends in all the high places. Unfortunately, it's a story he has a lot of history with. It's a subject that hits home with a lot of folks. Of course, time is of the essence. There is only a certain time for this to happen. A unique window of opportunity. A sense of urgency is on the table. His DNA—lots of questions, no answers. Confusion and intensity are paramount. But a huge question faces our character:

Can he really do it?
What happens if he really does it?
Is he ready to step outside himself?

Does he go along with the system? Brown noise again? Who wants to get burnt again? Is it possible to smell French

Roast coffee and a sweet rose during the same walk? Will he ever be able to escape his own madness? Will he find someone who understands him? Will life change if he starts believing his own words?

Intermittently
No intention
No understanding
We come up short of
What we wanted from the start
Short on being in a "sweet" spot
Short on feeling like we've gone somewhere
Besides an old habit
Creeping back to grab our tails
Wrenching new pain, from an old happening
Short on feeling something different
Short of knowing something about
What's around a corner, discovering
What we can become
What we really
Want not for today, but for
Tomorrow and the time after
Tomorrow
Away, from so many thoughts
Beyond an aura

Until I hear from you. You have my kindness, consideration, and forbearance.

Love + Peace,
Bill

Sub: Continuing
Date: 3/7/0011:15:59 PM Eastern Standard Time
From: NYCblackout
To: LEHUFF67

I haven't finished with you yet. Have you eaten? Sounds familiar?

Arc you happy to be away from Atlanta, USA.? Do you feel lighter, being away from American ideas and standards of reality? Are you happier being away from me? Are you feeling free? Are you getting content with your new surroundings? Have you met your new count? Are you comfortable?

If you are, you don't have to let me know. It's your time to find out to discover what is essential for you. You don't need any strings, obligations, roadblocks, or hesitations.

It was as if I left that you're also free to come back to our spot. Where element occurs. Where our imagination crafts an alternate reality. Where we find solace. Where it's all, we want it to be.

Until I hear from you. You have my.

Love,
Bill

Sub: Dealing
Date: 3/8/00 1 :49:42 AM Eastern Standard Time
From: NYCblackout
To: LEHUFF67

After I wrote you, I got a phone call from a girl Maria, a Brazilian girl I used to date. She was on the way over to the apartment. She wanted me to move in with her. She talked about hot plans to go to Brazil next month. All of this happened after I wrote you. I asked her to leave. She brushed me off and left. There was nothing to talk about.

I jot this down to you to let you know about my process over here. Obstacles other folks that may not want us to continue building. I can feel your touch right now. It's like you've never gone away. I'm waiting for you—hoping to feel more sprinkles from our magic.

I'm comfortable with our connection.

Bill

Sub: Hearing…Anticipating…
Date: 03/10/00 1:13:25 AM Eastern Standard Time
From: NYCblackout
To: LEHUFF67

How did you know before me? I'm glad. So happy to be awakened by your spirit. It's becoming all right. The long nights don't seem so lengthy as they were last week. Treachery dissipates, days shed, and isolation covers my moods. I'm waiting, working, imagining, and praying that all will be well.

Constantly. Ever more. You're all over my mind. I'm in love with your vibrations. Your essence. Your aura. Your inclination to fly away. Your returning presence, as time unfolds. Uniting your love, power and spirit—under a single canopy.

You're the first human I've escaped with. Nothing compares to these moments. Our time on earth. Our talking time in person, on the telephone, telepathy, seconds, minutes, and hours @ time. Observing. Contemplating. Listening to quiet. This separation requires us to be our own healer. Our own doctor. Healing comes from within. Nutrients to resolve stand right in front of us. It's only a matter of time.

What are you feeling? Are you settling in? Are you adjusting to mood, reflection, landscape, food, people, and movement? Should I stop writing? Should I stop thinking about you? Should I forget we ever meet?

Again, I'm wishing, meditating, and praying that our Creator walks in your every footstep. My meditation centers around our maker's decision, to watch over your smallest wish, need, and desire. I'm hoping that whatever you're hoping for, emerges as a clear vision before it actually happens. I really hope that you're now as happy, as you've ever been on earth.

Until I hear from you. You have my peace.

Bill

Sub: Accepting
Date: 3/10/0010:15:04 PM Eastern Standard Time
From: NYCblackout
To: LEHUFF67

There's lots of activities going on. Car horns blowing. CNN glaring all over town. The Hawks score a basket every now and then. Time moves forward. The past sustains a glimpse of wonder. People walk by my apartment. I can hear a strong wind in the mix. A melancholy sky. Sometimes, I hear people arguing through the walls. Yet nothing really happen without your presence. Your fire—igniting a dark spot.

Feelings can actually take place in a laboratory. Is it all about an experiment—up and down, in and out, round and round, with and without? Where a feeling may be a concoction or a figment of imagination. Something that nobody believes in, besides you. Nobody understands but you. You're trying to make something happen. You're attempting to do something out of the ordinary. Is there any meaning to your dreams, besides your own thoughts?

One day in South Carolina, I walked through an old church yard passing by tombstones and grave markers. I kept wondering who was under the markers. Some names were completely eroded. Other names were barely visible. We're talking late 1800s and early 1900s times on earth. What did they do before they arrived on earth? What were some of their experiences while on earth? Was there a connection between their dreams and hopes? Where are they now? Are they ok? An odd feeling crossed my mind. Is there anybody out there thinking about them now?

Hope all is well. Strong and moving toward a miniature destiny. Heart, soul, and spirit merging openly to receiving your essentials.

Until I hear from you.

Peace.

Bill

Sub: Timing
Date: 03/11/00 11: 28:55 PM Eastern Standard Time
From: NYCblackout
To: LEHUFF67

Is there any sense of timing when things happen? A manner in which they so happen. Sheer coincidence as to who they happened to. The relationship between being ready and accepting a peculiar situation. An inquiry into consequences. What would it be like and so on? Hey, I'm just wondering about our situation. Some mess you got us in.

I'm in love with the thought of you being alive. Your eyes slowly opening up, as an early morning sun creeps through and past a wooden window shutter. Your moves toward the future, stepping calmly away from fear.

I'm thinking about loving you for a long time. Yet I realize it could be short. Is it a delusion that we're physically separated? Yet we merge and unite via an unseen energy. Bending, twisting, and navigating through obstacles. Folks better get out of the way!

I don't like being away from you. It's way too lonely. During the day, it's too dark. At night, it's way too gloomy. At other times, I can see my own shadow. It's a quarry of madness. Tossed and tangled up with murky feelings. On the other hand, I'm aware of your sensitivity. Emoting, coming, and radiating from another side. Projecting a knowledge of the whole matter. That everything will be all right. That I'm not alone, stumbling along a path on my way over there.

For sure, I happen to love you madly. It shouts out like a wild brush fire. Caught up in a late summer windstorm spreading flames.

Until I hear more signals.

Bill

Sub: Re: Dealing
Date: 03/13/00 2:02:53 PM Eastern Standard Time
From: LEHUFF67
To: NYCblackout

So, Bill,

What's wrong with Brazil, anyway?

I don't want you to wait for something you can get in Brazil. I can't even begin to digest all you have writen.

Bill, where the hell did you come from and why? And can you explain it to me? Like I told you today on the phone, you are my only friend. What would I do without you?

What I have learned from you about patience and love?

You should know you and your love, your constant love made this all happen.

Good god almighty.

You should have Maria and Brazil or whoever else comes along go take it. Do you understand me? Am I making any sense? Does it make sense, no. None of this makes sense. I cannot tell you. You are an incredible person. And I am grateful to know you and to have learned so much form you, and of course I care about you and love you very much. What I am saying is, do what you need to do if you need to do it. I am just feeling like I need to say this one more time.

So I said it. Now. Get to work. Move it.

Where are you? What do I do now? What am I going to do? I want for you to be happy and successful and safe and warm and working. I will be thinking of you and knowing you are thinking of me. And thank you for saving my life again today. Thank you for being my friend and for caring and knowing and thinking.

Lee

Connecting Up

Sub: Re: Missing you again
Date: 03/13/00 2:09:08 PM Eastern Standard Time
From: LEHUFF67
To: NYCblackout

Bill,

What are we to do? Where does this come from? I don't know what to say. You are overwhelming me. You have overwhelmed me. I don't know what to say. It is so much. So much.

Are you sure you want to give it to me? How about your dreams? I am not trying to upset, just figure it out. I can't figure it out.

Lee

Sub: Coming back
Date: 03/15/00 12:32:01 AM Eastern Standard Time
From: NYCblackout
To: LEHUFF67

That distance we were apart turns out not to be so distant after all. I didn't have to reach that far to embrace a warm radiance, a golden sun shine, zooming around your forehead. Traveling up my spine and curving over next to my heart. Eliminating what was cloudy, shaky, dangerous, and scary. Suddenly a breeze cooled things off, placing me close to an image of a tall tree—one that touches the sky, early in the morning.

For sure, this is not a time for jive games, threats, innuendos, or suspended animations. So I'm back at a similar spot. The time before confusion set in. It's like this with what's going down. Under this, you want me to sell out for a one-night stand? I'm on a mission. It doesn't call for any more diversions.

Do you think distance or geography would do anything to affect what was growing prior to perception? An energy flows in a straight space. It's almost as if I detect, what you're thinking. What you imagine. What you're feeling—reservations, doubts, hopes, and anticipation. Immediately before one of your dreams unfold. I really can't call it.

Similar to lucidity. Closer to mellow. It takes over every step I make. I can't go anywhere without thinking about you. Every move I take is a dance with you. Constantly. Vibrantly. Very lightly. Softly. You make up an entire special collection floor of the New York Public Library on 5th Avenue when it comes to feelings. Your sign is excellent, distinguishable, and delicate.

I see it everywhere I go. While it's vast, I don't understand, all your love. I'm not sure how you feel about me. I really don't know if you love me. Yet I know you care. Sometimes, I feel you want to go and hide away from me. I can't help it; my mind wanders as much as my fingers search and point. I'm not even close to an area where I can feel all your warmth.

Is it really possible to move beyond the past—the pain of being denied—a cold shoulder of neglect? Is this when you see light at the end of the tunnel? It is coming to term with a trouble thought. Somehow to summon a lost courage to wrap our brain around. Regardless of the odds. I'm going to make it. After the dust settles, the rain stops. And although it's dark outside/inside, I'm comforted. I'm sufficient. I'm cool with my surroundings. I'm ok with waiting for you.

I hope peace travels with you - each step/increment of your journey and your family and friends.

Bill

Sub: Gleeful
Date: 03/16/00 12:00:40 AM Eastern Standard Time
From: NYCblackout
To: LEHUFF67

I will never forget you no matter where you sit. Any place you travel. An area code. An oblique telephone number. An unrecognizable e-mail addresses. Wherever you sleep. Trailing all this is a mirage—a feeling.

Your power. Your image. Your sensate that unique sound of your pulse. Then there's a solitude about twinkle, near your eye. Just between them, is a ring of your memory. Recalling a reflection of revelation - our movements. Quite unpredictable. Hanging deeply, wallowing and listening to each other's signal. I don't have a struggle when it comes to being near you. It's a blessing that I'm learning more about everyday. I'm growing to appreciate you more as time passes. I'm grateful to touch a circle, harboring your energy.

I have love, for you.

I'm falling, way over my head.

Yet I'm even happier about our future. A book. A new story. A film. Hanging out in a space where exploration is kin to awakening, where faith walks besides the weary on the way to a golden sunrise. A happy moment. A triumph over adversity. Reclaiming a lost spirit—all take place under a notion. Close by two hearts showing off, like they've known each other since day one.

My love for you has grown. I can't tell the difference between magic and reality. I don't have a clue. All I know is that it covers all that I see. It's imbedded in any street I cross. Passing under traffic lights. Around each curve on the road of life, Your love bears a tender mood, a comfort spot. Each experience is not far from the previous one. Every feeling is just like it's taking place, under my thumb.

Your sensation is spreading. At the same time, I'm bewildered. It's difficult to deny that what you want to happen, will be happening soon. Our only struggle is to resist, putting things in terms of the outside, physical world. It is natural for the mind to react to two forces: what we feel inside and/or what our eyes see on the outside. When you're dreaming, your eyes are closed to the outside world. When you're creating, your soul is busy on its own.

Until I hear more of your signal. I'll continue to work, gravitate more and closer to where probable, meets up with possible. Where fear is missing. I love how your love forms up, gels, coalesces—larger that what an eye detects.

Peace.

Bill

Sub: Closer to U
Date: 03/17/00 5:31:02 PM Eastern Standard Time
From: NYCblackout
To: LEHUFF67

It's been only a few moments since we hung up. Your sigh still rings in my ear as we talked about, tucking you in, patting you on the head, making sure everything was all right. It felt just like I was standing at your bedside. Actually, positioning your pillow, tucking you in, and patting your head. Wonderful.

I'm feeling closer to you these past few hours. It seems we went thru a dark tunnel. We did it together separately, and now we're out. Right now, we can see sunshine, clearing fog and falling obstacles. There seems to be slight movement up our ladder toward dreams, over to destiny. I'm glad you're close.

I hope you get some good rest. Your dreams are clearer. Closer to your fingertips, comfortable in the palm of your hand. I'm wishing that peace watches over your journey. Yet I don't want you to leave. Yes, travel anywhere. Explore your heart's desire. Touch down where you may. Do a necessary thing. But don't go anywhere—beyond our spot.

Bill

Sub: Re: Gleeful
Date: 3/18/00 4:59:49 AM Eastern Standard Time
From: LEHUFF67
To: NYCblackout

Rosemary is growing.

It's not easy to understand. It's not. It just is.

I don't understand much, but I think you are the one. This is your doing.

Thank you for showing me so much love and respect and for being so much to me and for me.

No matter what time of the day or night—there you are always there. No matter what.

Thank you for being.

Lee

Sub: Re: Closer.U
Date: 03/18/00 4:05:44 AM Eastern Standard Time
From: LEHUFF67
To: NYCblackout

I did need to use pulse tone on both modem/properties and AOL set up, but I did it!

I can't imagine that you are amazed by me, whatever does this mean. I must say that you are the one who made this happen; it's not me at all. Not me at all. It does seem that you were tucking me in. I have in you so much love and security, the guardian, the safe harbor. And you, you put up with so much from me. Why?

Are you sleeping? I just got on line, if you call and it's busy.

Lee

Sub: Excellent
Date: 3/18/00 9:30:53 AM Eastern Standard Time
From: NYCblackout
To: LEHUFF67

One can imagine a comfortable feeling to embrace an escalating and flowing tide of emotions. All riding a wave of awe. Pondering love.

Excellent is how it feels, thinking about you. Our dreams. Hopes. Tapestry of moods. I get a groove when I detect our embroidery. Coming full circle. Mingling with art. Destiny. Fate. How you share your soul.

It seems insufficient to say thank you.

Much is how I love you.

Bill

Sub: Encompassing
Date: 03/19/00 9:32:50 AM Eastern Standard Time
From: NYCblackout
To: LEHUFF67

Sugar & Spice Screenplay completed, 06/99. Production Budget Estimate 09/99. Screen Partners forty percent (40%) commitment 10-11/99. Leona Elizabeth Huff connection, 12/99. Regal Theaters Distribution negotiations (Donald Jordan), 03/06/00 & Vienna Film Fund Application Completion, 03/21/00.

So I'm not afraid of the process. I'm only afraid of the people involved in the process—the Vern's & Kay's of the world. Are they going to keep their word? Will they be faithful to their word? But I need to step back a minute and check out my own feelings. This will give me a chance to examine if there's anything that I'm putting up to prevent the wheels from turning.

I just talked to Wolfgang. I told him that I had completed the translation, and that FedEx is estimated to deliver on Thursday. He confirmed that he'd look everything over and let me know what's missing and what we would need to do to next. If you didn't know it yet, this is a long, scary, and complicated game.

I'm excited about your new discoveries. I called you this morning. No answer. Your voice was the first thing I wanted to hear. I yearn to hear you laugh out loud. Those telling vibrations from your sounds when we talk. Your silence. Your echo. I'm missing that particular ring, an image of you.

Bill

Sub: On the way over
Date: 3/19/00 12: 12:29 AM Eastern Standard Time
From: NYCblackout
To: LEHUFF67

I'm tired. I'm sleepy, anxious, glad, and happy that Thomas came over. He was angry about what happened to him. Like in one of those Sherlock Holmes mysteries when a sweet girl dumps the guy. How could this have happened to my buddy Thomas? What could he have done differently? Why didn't she tell him earlier? After talking things through, he came to the conclusion that if she didn't love him. There was nothing that he could have done different.

So after all this, we ate and got down to business. It's business that I have to concentrate on the next two days. I'm going to work tonight. There's tons of paperwork, but I know Wolfgang. Once he gets our package, he'll be able to place in the right hand that's the only way to get to the next part of the journey.

Now we know what's on the table: appreciation, patience, urging, gumption, and energy throughout a hassle, hang up, uncertainty, and intensity. I've been thinking since we talked today. I've been thinking about Vienna too, you and being over there with you.

My love makes a way. A path to you, aimlessly. It's not a concoction or a notion. It goes beyond words or phrases. Until l hear from you, I'm wishing that peace continues to visit with you, Big Momma, Maggie, and all of your family.

Until,
Bill

Sub: Re: On the way over
Date: 3/19/00 4:16:31 AM Eastern Standard Time
From: LEHUFF67
To: NYCblackout

Well, I told you there would be therapy.

So it's all done, the translation? Another delay, what are you dragging your feet for? It's fine, but perhaps you might take some time to look at the situation. Maybe there are some issues you are not aware of as of yet, that you are not addressing. Yes, you need to sleep.

I have been practicing my poses and faces! Maybe, this is what I have been meaning to do. Maybe. I am certain I have the ability. I thought about what you said; you should try it. Maybe this is it. I've tried this and that and the other. Maybe this is it. Today, I am going to Todi and Orvieto. Many Americans live in Todi—I am told.

And you work today? Why not tomorrow? Try and think about the speed issue. I think it is possible there maybe something you are not looking at fear of success. Maybe. You should spend some time with though. Get it out of the way. Because there is something in the way. I think.

What did you eat? Maggie and Big Mama—that's wonderful for you to think of them. Thank you. Ok get to work. Get to sleep. Eat well. I will be thinking about you.

Lee

Sub: Coloring
Date: 3/19/00 11:06:15 PM Eastern Standard Time
From: NYCblackout
To: LEHUFF67

Like a lot of people I've known or thought I knew, I'm drawn to the dark side of town. The other side of the tracks is a place we all like to visit. Some stay and others have no choice, except to stay. Others go back when they think, nobody is looking. Ok. I like danger, and I'm lost, just when I think I'm found.

For a long time, I've had a feeling that I was someone else other than myself, like I was born in a dark place, with lightness just around the corner. Ever since I can remember, I kept feeling that the world was like a dry land—waiting for a drop of rain to come.

One could wonder about raindrop. How long it took Michelangelo to finish "David?" What did he struggle with, to prevent him from finishing up so quickly? Was he in a rush to finish? Did he take time to unravel what was essential to merging spirit, heart and soul? Later on, this would be revealed through his fingertips. I'm not sure of your comment, and I've got to go because it's lightening. But I wanted to share something with you.

I'm after an essence. An understanding on existence. I feel like a piece of clay—shaped by circumstance and imagination.

I'm not seeking a podium to shout-out barbs on how it is to love, hate, destroy, kill, or injure. We're hoping to forge a feeling about a certain situation that has existed way before we've come to know the current situation (nuclear war, materialism, possession, ownership, and locking oneself into concrete). Our characters are those folks who examine a peculiar feeling. It's the kind of feeling you get when you follow a thought, without knowing.

Please, stay strong on your book. Keep your own vigil. Be aware of your movements. I'm also hoping that peace is your refuge. Whenever you have doubts or reservations. You could get a charge by looking inside at something, anything, you can't see.

Until I hear your signals, I remain with you.

Love,
Bill

Sub: Re: a ggn
Date: 3/20/00 1:48:32 PM Eastern Standard Time
From: LEHUFF67
To: NYCblackout

A mile high sign.

It is good for us not to speak.

However, I don't have much to write. I've thought of you once or twice today. So where are you now?

I'll see you later, a presto.

Ciao.

Sub: Re: a ggn
Date: 3/20/00 1:57:32 PM Eastern Standard Time
From: NYCblackout
To: LEHUFF67

So it's really good. I bet. It's good, and it's not too good. But it's also an opportunity to know more about something that I'm not sure yet.

Yet I'm finding out. I'm discovering more about a feeling. It's sticking to me like early morning dew on green grass like white, on rice, a cat's meow, and like a butterfly, landing softly. Flopping wings and extracting nectar. Yet the flower feels familiar.

Love you much.

Peace.

Bill

Sub: Aware
Date: 3/20/00 11:22:03 PM Eastern Standard Time
From: NYCblackout
To: LEHUFF67

I'm looking around the apartment, listening to Mazy Starr. I'm exploring ridges of love you left behind. Those little quiet things, only you do. Your touch, lingers.

I'm aware of your love. I can't figure out why my heart skips a beat. Is it the love you took away? Is it the love you left behind? I wonder why you even left. You told me—you wanted to find something that was missing. You talked a lot about something you left behind in Italy. Have you found it?

I'm awed by you. You have space with me. You can bet it's not an area I created. I didn't carve anything out. It's all your doing. You made a way into my heart. Our space is mutual. It's our creation. No agenda. No hassles. No other invitations. Nobody knows. Duality in place. Untouchable.

Every time, my thoughts about you center on unison, a oneness. Without pretense. Without interruption. I like how it feels to be near you. I've never imagined such a feeling, where everything is new. A fresh feeling. A sensation of hope. Exceeding promise. I'm missing you, right now. I'll be up all night putting paperwork for tomorrow's FedEx to Vienna. Another part of our future begins. I trust you. I feel your love creeping all over the place.

Until I hear more of your sign, I'll be waiting for you up on deck—where our heads look to an open sky. Watching a baby seagull on an early morning flight. Winging it over choppy waters. Soaring high. Descending low, then high again. Gaining confidence. Each nudge sustains another shot of courage. As the seagull soars, our fingers connect beyond a distant horizon.

I'm praying that peace continues to visit with you, Big Momma, Maggie, Dan & Sue, your cousins, and all the other folks you love.

Bill

Sub: Re: Aware
Date: 3/21/00 6:14:06 AM Eastern Standard Time
From: LEHUFF67
To: NYCblackout

I find what you say and know and communicate to me incredibly fantastic and magical. There is nothing left out or misplaced or forgotten. You are most incredible extraordinary remarkable. I feel your love with every line you write. Every word you choose.

How can it be that you are in awe of me? My talent is overshadowed by your gifts for expression. Feeling what you say, saying what you feel. How odd that we connected. You must know that you have made this happen. I have been at the crossroads with you many times. Forget about it! And then you come at me with more love and kindness, and I would have to say out loud Holy Cow! God Damn It.

I don't know exactly what definition covers this. I don't know how it fits together. I still feel the pull and twist of society, I must be honest. It is very difficult for me. To allow this relationship to be more than friendship. And yet, can it be that? And only that? How would it be for you? If I took a lover? Found a count? Married a pirate and sailed the seven seas?

Tell me. What do I know and believe? Is that we both care for and have love for the other. And, yes, love doesn't drop by that often. Sometimes, not at all. And you must know that you have taught me what it is to be loved. You have given me so much in the face of selfishness and fear. You continued to love me beyond measure when I do not deserve your love at all. So it's you. All of you.

I often think it impossible that another could ever express, feel, give as much love as you. And as you well know, I am most often right. It is difficult for me to not know what this really is, and or what we think it is. Maybe, you should not give me so much love. Maybe, I should not take so much. Maybe, I don't give as much as you.

I don't want to be unfair to you. I don't want to be unkind to you. I think you know of the struggle I face. Perhaps, I am not strong enough. Perhaps, your love is more deserving of another—someone more older than me. Someone who could give you everything that you have dreamed of. What I am trying to do is be honest with you. Perhaps, the time has come to confront the issue. I want to be straight. Getting it straight. Understand. Know. This is where I am. And what do you think? You truly deserve so much more than me. You do.

Tell me what you think. Tell me how you feel. I hope you got all of your work done and that you had a good sleep.

Lee

Sub: CHANGE
Date: 3/21/00 8:55:53 AM Eastern Standard Time
From: NYCblackout
To: LEHUFF67

Yes, there is this ongoing hassle in society about relationships—straight, gay, transgender, or weird? It's all about drawing a circle around a relationship and stating if one and one don't equal two, we can't let you join our club. If you're black and your partner is white, or if you not straight, you better watch out.

I've had a little of it on my own, with invitations to go south with Maria. Then too, the current physical separation allows an opportunity to take on a lover or two for you. Have a bunch of romantic encounters in small skiing villages and cities near the Alps. I know the moments are there for you to be taken away or get taken.

How does all of this feel? Unusual. Less than cool. Awkward. Unacceptable. If you decided to take on a lover, I'd have to deal with that. You have a right to do what you want. It would be unrealistic to deny you anything. You're free as the air you breathe. What I'm trying to say is that I feel so out of place with other people. Lacking. Inadequate. Even in a crowd of folks, your face is all I see.

When I tell you, "you're on my mind"
That's missing the point
You're actually deeper
You're living with me
I go to bed with you on my mind
When I toss and turn
I feel you lying next to me
Sometimes
I holler your name out, in the dark of night

During slumber, a ringing pulsation points in your direction
And when I wake up, it's like your touch
Alerting me that it's Ok to get up
That we're on the way to something beyond

Somewhere down deep, you and my soul made company. A sacred spot. Words come up short. I do a poor job on description.

I'm drawn to your magic. My love belongs near you. I only want things to be right for you. I want you to be happy. I respect you. My love stretches out, over a border.

If you choose to tell me, that's all right. If you choose not to tell me, that's all right too. I'll understand. Does that answer your question? I don't know if I've done a good job with your question. I'm letting you know my feelings.

There's a lot that I feel from you: compassion, consideration, kindness, sensations, and resonance from your eyes. It just wouldn't be the same with a stranger.

You're free to experiment in order to find out. Anytime. Anywhere. Always. Free to navigate any space. Geography. Countries. Continents. Freedom resides with you, not attached to any other human or permission. As a spirit, you arrive on earth with freedom and power. You can run all over your own kingdom. It might be selfish, self-centered or even crazy, but I just want you to run to me.

This territory is new. Our feelings are not connected to words. This is a place we've never been. So it's scary.

Bill

Sub: Being strong
Date: 3/23/00 9:17:20 AM Eastern Standard Time
From: NYCblackout
To: LEHUFF67

Being strong is not the word it sounds like. It's like being who you are and who you want to be. It's a feeling of being surrounded by a ferocious alligator in the Louisiana swamps. Whatever I say to you, I must do also. When I tell you, "be strong," I must in turn show my strength. It's not idle talk or Philosophy 301.

Last night, I got a call from the South American girl again. The first words out of her mouth, "I miss you terribly." I had to tell her no again. Nobody is going to know why I'm saying no to them. This is my business. I'm not comparing somebody else to you. Remember when I told you I had no response to your request for me to take *x* or *y* on the other night we were on the phone.

No, way. There's no comparison. There's nothing or no one to put up against what we have and share. Your love is beyond anything—everything I've thought about or felt seems possible. Your courage is imbedded down deep. Your gentleness is bountiful, planted, bending, meandering thru and over my heart.

Being nervous is ok. When I write to you, I'm nervous as to what I'm going to say. What I will say. It's the same when I'm writing a story or script. Being scared and sweating it out is cool. It is an energy, an inertia. Is there a difference between anger and passion? Is an angry lover more involved than a passionate lover?

Nervous energy. Frightful. Being afraid. Waking up in the middle of the night. Sweating nerves could be a source of emotion to let our character speak her own mind. Let the hair down. Kick up some dirt. It could be a reason to step up to the plate and not strike out. Being in this spot, allows a certain freedom to slide into a next phase. It could be a flow over to an ancient truth, a family secret, a treasure of insights not only in your character's pituitary gland but within our hearts. A heart that used to be known for rapid beats and rushing.

I believe in your purpose, your character, your energy, your faith, your will, and your sweet love. Until I hear more of your signals, you have my.

Peace,
Bill

Sub: With U
Date: 3/23/00 10:58:02 PM Eastern Standard Time
From: NYCblackout
To: LEHUFF67

A brief second. A long moment. Escalating hours. Lengthy days. Slow dwindling nights. I'm advancing to accept phenomena. An unbelievable notion about your love.

Nothing is missing from your love. Cascading toward me. Hooking up to rolling thunderstorms. A lightning strike from the other side of a rainbow. Something's just over the hill top.

I love you more than a word. I can't come up with a word that comes close to fleeting. Nothing is left behind. I love your eyes. I love your nose. I love the space between your eyes. I'm attracted to the crevice of your lips. I love the curves on your brow (is it big or small, I forget sometime). I'm in love with your soul and how it fades into spirit. I happen to love your personality and how it stretches to enlightenment.

I happen to be with you—all the time. I can't imagine ever leaving. My love lingers on a loose limb, near you.

Bill

Date: 03/26/00 3:48: 11 AM Eastern Standard Time
From: NYCblackout
To: LEHUFF67

So much is coming together. So many things, presented. A ton of unfolding, peeling away old hang-ups. Shedding old jive. Unraveling over yonder. Geography no longer matters. Near where I stand is a warm feeling. It's a good feeling to know you. You're all over the map. Now, you're touching me again.

AIR BILL # 8188 1162 7808

TO: LEONA ELIZABETH HUFF FLORENCE, ITALY

POSTAL CODE. 50100 LOCAL FedEx # 800. 123.800

DIRECTIONS TO FedEx STATION: @ VIA GOBEM N #3 CAMPI BISENZIO

FROM ALL EXITS TO PRATO EST, TURN RIGHT TO CAMPI BISENZJO, ACROSS (CROSS) THE BRIDGE, FOLLOW THE ROAD, AND TURN @ THE SIGN (?)

Oh well! Let me know when you receive your goodie package from FedEx or how you like everything. I hope the socks warm your feet. I'm experiencing a love directed toward you, which grows everyday, every hour. As I think about you, it takes on a different depth, perceives a fresh signal, indicating there's so much more to come.

Ciao.

I love you.

Bill

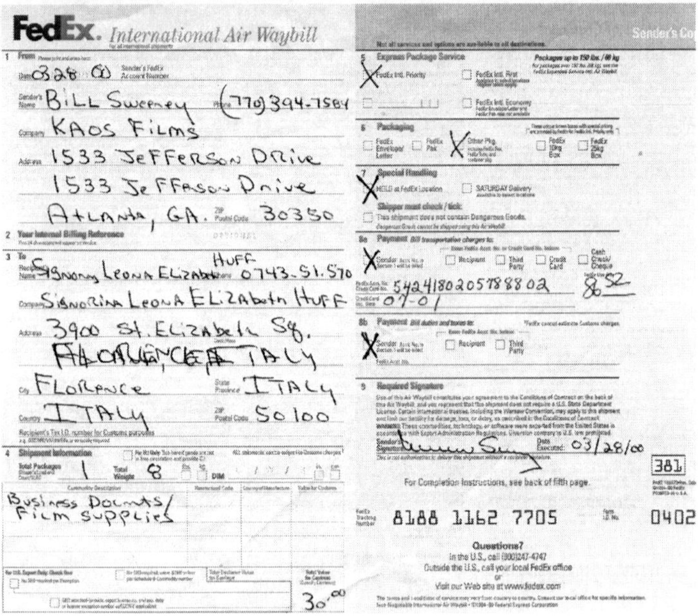

FedEx. International Air Waybill

1 From
Date 03 28 00 Sender's FedEx Account Number
Sender's Name BiLL Sweeney Phone (770) 394-7584
Company KAOS FiLms
Address 1533 JeFFeRSoN DRive
1533 JeFFason Drive
AtLANtA, GA. ZIP Postal Code 30350

2 Your Internal Billing Reference

3 To
Recipient's Name Signorina Leona Elizabeth HUFF Phone 0743-51.570
Company SiGNoRiNA LeoNA ELiZAbeth HUFF
Address 3900 St. ELiZAbeth Sq.
FLORENCE, ITALY
City FLoRence State Province ITALY
Country ITALY ZIP Postal Code 50100
Recipient's Tax I.D. number for Customs purposes

4 Shipment Information
Total Packages 1 Total Weight 8
Commodity Description: Business Documents/ Film supplies
Total Value for Customs: 30.00

Not all services and options are available to all destinations.

5 Express Package Service — Packages up to 150 lbs. / 68 kg
X FedEx Intl. Priority
FedEx Intl. First
FedEx Intl. Economy

6 Packaging
FedEx Envelope/ Letter
FedEx Pak
X Other Pkg.
FedEx 10kg Box
FedEx 25kg Box

7 Special Handling
X HOLD at FedEx Location
SATURDAY Delivery
Shipper must check / tick:
This shipment does not contain Dangerous Goods.

8a Payment Bill transportation charges to:
X Sender
Recipient
Third Party
Credit Card
Cash/ Check/ Cheque
FedEx Acct. No. / Credit Card No. 5424180205788802
86.52
Credit Card Exp. Date 07-01

8b Payment Bill duties and taxes to:
X Sender
Recipient
Third Party

9 Required Signature
Sender's Signature
Date Executed: 03/28/00

381

For Completion Instructions, see back of fifth page.

FedEx Tracking Number 8188 1162 7705 Form I.D. No. 0402

Questions?
In the U.S., call (800)247-4747
Outside the U.S., call your local FedEx office
or
Visit our Web site at www.fedex.com

FedEx International Air Waybill Ticket
Photograph on 3/28/00

Sub: THERE -NOW
Date: 03/28/00 10:24:36 AM Eastern Standard Time
From: NYCblackout
To: LEHUFF67

I've been struggling all week. Maybe it all started last Saturday at Old Navy. It all jumped out as the chick behind the counter asked, "Is this for your wife? Scared as a dog, I said it was for my girl friend. Really, I've been tussling with myself. Trying to put my finger on why the feeling was so lame.

Still to this hour, I can't really tell you what's going on besides an isolated vibe that takes me farther away from you. While a mellow beat brings me back, right next to your heart. My love for you is endless. My hope is to learn more about it. My other hope is to understand how to give you more. How to share more with you now. How to be in space with you. How to love you differently. I happen to love you more than ever. Right now.

I love how you love me. It's what I've been waiting for. Never knew it would come. Never thought about it happening in this lifetime. Use to wish that God grant a moment to let people who love each other actually take time time to love each other. Along side this wish is that the love could nurture without barriers or interruptions.

Ciao,
Bill

Sub: All right, now
Date: 3/29/00 8: 50: 19 AM Eastern Standard Time
From: NYCblackout
To: LEHUFF67

I was just listening to NPR's Morning Edition. There was a story about Seattle's commerce, computers and art hanging out together. There's a little town across the bay, and you can only get there by ferry. There's no industry. Local folks just want to learn computers and hit the road for Seattle. They depend on Seattle for everything. So there's this lady who owns an old house. She recently renovated. Now she's renting rooms out to artists, painters, puppetry makers—developing their own world, focusing, creating, and working on some small dreams. Then she said, "I think we're in the 3rd Act of a three-act play. And we'll be so happy when all the performers do their own thing. We'll be applauding."

I thought about you so much last night, when I was making the cookies. I felt you around, the kitchen. It seemed as though you were watching to see if the cookies were ready. Could you have put in the flour and me the butter? Is it really, a play on words. Is it just one person doing the action? Is it the power of 2 souls who became conscious? A lot of times, I feel alone with you. In harmony with you. In sync with you but not hanging around earth or space. It's almost as if we're incognito.

Then too, is it eligible for a label or category. Can it even fit definition? Could it be a long walk or something? A long country ride? A journey thru life? Where we're sharing a blessing to learn, grow, strip away barriers? Could it be an opportunity to explore another stage of existence?

Where our past is but a memory where walls that prevented fullness, crumble as we walk by. Where, if we waver or have doubts, faith creates a limb to catch our fall, reaching out and grabbing us, just before we hit bottom. Where all visions, images, and feelings we anticipated are not only exceeded but connect to an openness, frankness, a hidden unique. All that we ever wanted drifts closer to our outstretched hands.

Some goodies will be at the FedEx Station @ CAMPI BISENZIO on Friday, March 31, 2000, waiting for you to come by. I'll e-mail you an air bill #.

You got my heart in your hand.

Bill

Sub: 1111111111/I111
Date: 03/31/00 7:21:23 AM Eastern Standard Time
From: NYCblackout
To: LEHUFF67

I really hope that your move to Florence works out. The logistics of getting there. Moving there and settling down seem heavy.

The difficult I'll do now. The impossible will take a little while longer.

Until I hear your signal.

Peace.

Bill

Sub: Re: 1/II11111/II111
Date: 3/31/00 3:29:44 PM Eastern Standard Time
From: LEHUFF67
To: NYCblackout

What is that subject suppose to mean?
Where are you hiding?
Call me.
I am leaving here in 6 hours.

Lee

Sub: Re: Wondering
Date: 4/2/00 2:50: 14 PM Eastern Daylight Time
From: LEHUFF67
To: NYCblackout

Hey! What are you doing? What are you thinking about? Why are you questioning me? My decisions to be here, to do what I have set out to do? Why?

I have expressed my need for space, for a non-intensive relationship. Have I been unable to express myself? Have I been unable to communicate? What I am saying is not understood?

Yes, we have an uncommon, rare connection. Yes, I realize the beauty and uniqueness of that. I care for and love you as a human being, as a friend. You have been so incredibly generous to me with your time, your knowledge, your thoughts, your insight. I have been comforted by all of your gifts. I have found strength and courage in your words and deeds. I have grown because of you. I have become more of who I am. I'm anchored in a safe harbor.

As we continue to move into the future, I have felt confined in the past weeks. Contained. I love you but am not in love with you. I love your patience, your caring, nurturing spirit, your undying, never failing being to be there.

I want to talk to you about things that happen to me and things that happen to you and how your film is and where my book is and what happens in the world and who said what to who and what happened then and where did it happen. I want. I need. I would like to have your friendship. For me, speaking all the time, speaking all the time about love and loving—I can't breathe. I can't.

This is too much for me. I apologize to you for not being able to receive, for not being able to be a receptor for all of your love. Please forgive me for allowing this to progress to this point. I have failed to communicate fully to you my feelings. I have not expressed fully to you. I am feeling the need for space, for clarity.

At this moment, and perhaps for all time, I do not see what you see for us. I am at a loss. We want different things from each other. And I do not want for you to continue to feel slighted, discounted. I care, I do love, but not in that way. Not the same as you. Romantic. Physical. No.

What do you want to do?

Tell me.

Lee

Sub: Wondering
Date: 4/2/00 9:34:56 AM Eastern Daylight Time
From: NYCblackout
To: LEHUFF67

So you've got a dream. You go away, in order for your dream to have life. Many European writers like Rilke and Solzhenitsyn did the same. James Baldwin left New York for Turkey and Paris. Josephine Baker left St. Louis for Paris, Jimi Hendrix left New York for London—they all found something bigger than themselves. Did Olga inspire Boris Pasternak's *Doctor Zhivago*? On the contrary, did Pasternak inspire Olga to create more intrinsic translations of foreign poets? An escape from madness could be a home for a dream. It's on this path that a dream finds its' core.

Nobody is running away from anything. You're leaving to discover. You're searching so you can find. You're throwing stuff away to allow something to enter. Yet you're not concerned with the trip. All you're doing is traveling and roaming. All the other stuff is what the other folks talk about.

Yes, I've been angry @ you for a cold shoulder. I've been pissed off (last week) at your denial of love, coming your way. But I haven't stopped loving you. I haven't stopped sensing your signal. I'm still waiting for your love to grow more. My prayer and hope are the same—that your love blossoms.

Above all, it's caused me to sense a deeper appreciation of your essence, glow, radiance—our spot where independently, we dwell as two and live as one. Where all of what we feel thrives fully, as your palm rests in my hand. Where what we believe, hope for, receives vitality from our connection.

Bill

Sub: Merging
Date: 4/3/00 8:43:32 AM Eastern Daylight Time
From: NYCblackout
To: LEHUFF67

Since you called this morning, my mind, soul, body, and spirit have been merging around an identical spot—ours.

There's nothing I can wish except to move out of the way of our energy. Not to disturb it. Not to dictate how it could be. Even what it should be. I'm overwhelmed with its power to go beyond what I see or feel. Each time, the word love arises, you're nearby. You're behind it. You're just above it. You're side by side. Look around, and you're just underneath. Even while you're close at hand.

Yesterday must have been about some kind of healing. Something was thrown away and replaced with our understanding. Maybe I learned to trust you more. Maybe I learned to stay away from you. It just felt like something was healed. A bridge was crossed. Now, there's no anger. Only more acceptance. More tolerance. More love.

In Africa, when a child learns to fully wash their hands, they're considered clean. Then they're allowed to sit with the adults and eat at the same table. You get a sense that you have to be clean or pure, to move up in the world. This provides an insight into accepting another frame of understanding. Existing at another level. Quietly, your perspectives are not so remote from reality.

That is how it felt yesterday. Being alone in a church, hearing prayers, seeing prayers answered. It was a vibe, like something had been taken away, and what arrived was pure happiness. I felt I had a right to be with you, that I wanted to work in harmony with you. It felt like my place was a place with you.

When I was going out the door yesterday, something odd happened. Your plant, the limb you brought over the last night you were here, started to fall down. I grabbed it and said to myself, *No, you're not falling down. You're still the one. You're the only one.* I'm just barely beginning to understand our love. Bear with me. Please be patient with me.

I said a prayer for you this morning. I prayed last night for your love before I went to bed. It was a prayer to God for watching over our every footstep. It was a request for guidance and directions as we move ahead. It was a reach for insights on what is really essential. Above all, it was silent hope for Grace to stay close by, as the long nights of doubt and those uneven days of uncertainty continue. Did you hear our prayer?

Bill

Sub: Yearning
Date: 4/4/00 12:58:55 AM Eastern Daylight Time
From: NYCblackout
To: LEHUFF67

I just got thru e-mailing Martin on our schedule for Cannes. It starts May 10–21, 2000 with a stop off in Vienna to blend Wolfgang's effort with the Vienna Film Fund. On May 15–16, there will be an afternoon in Paris with Jean Luc (Music Lyrics & Soundtrack) & his cool wife and little boy. Then coffee with Pierre L'homme—our alternate cinematographer (he won a French Caesar Award, i.e. equivalent to an Academy Award for Camille Claudel) and a visit with Azzedine Alaia (advant-garde designer who loves to big butts, juggling up and under his Northern Italian silks and Tunisian cottons).

I'll set foot in Cannes on May 17, 2000. I left the door open for two to three days of unplanned meetings. Hopefully, all the meetings should be over in Cannes by late Friday, May 19, 2000. I told Martin that it's my fervent hope to get lost for seven/eight days in the food markets of Cannes. South France's flowers and eucalyptus are way beyond description. Some of them grow near where Picasso painted. When the fragrance comes near your nose, you almost feel like you help plant and nourished them. Yes, the food is excellent along with vino.

By knowing you, I've become stronger. I know a lot more about my feelings since I meet you. I'm closer to understanding myself since I meet you. You've generated a Major C change in confidence. I couldn't have made it this far without your encouragement and love. Actually, your love bobs and weaves like an old tapestry throughout my being, coming to rest at several spots, down deep in my soul.

Right now, I feel much love coming from you. Emanating from your spot, over there. Radiating and tumbling toward me. Nothing is rushed. Yet, it arrives fully and without notice. I want your love. I'm not ashamed to tell you know how much it means to me to share your love. I hope your rest was quiet and peaceful. I'm glad for you. Until I hear more of your signal, you have my wish for peace to continue visiting you, Big Momma, Maggie, Dan, & Sue.

Bill

Sub: Writing
Date: 4/4/00 8:34:23 AM Eastern Daylight Time
From: NYCblackout
To: LEHUFF67

This morning or last night, I had a dream about you.

You were talking to me. On the telephone. Or in person. We were away from where we are now. Suddenly, you started talking about an actress. Then you said, "Remember her? She would be right for this part." You said that you and a group or your staff had written a script with a special actress in it. Was she famous or was it you? It wasn't clear.

What was clear was your confidence. Your strength that you had decided to select a specific story and a particular actress. This actress maybe she was from a famous show. I faintly remember you saying something like that. Maybe it was your book or story, converted into a film script? So you made a decision to produce it. You had a staff or some other folks behind, doing grunt work.

My love for you is grown. Encompassing tons of confidence. So little fear. So much hope. A bunch of faith in each other, our dreams and our love. Please rest up today after your FedEx run.

Bill

Sub: Re: Writing
Date: 4/4/00 1:03:29 PM Eastern Daylight Time
From: LEHUFF67
To: NYCblackout

Thank you so much for all the goodies. The cookies are especially good. I can't wait to put my blue shirt on and listen to the tape of Andre. Even though the directions were cryptic to FedEx, I got there without having to turn around once!

It is raining cats and dogs again. I went to the grocery store and could not decide what to eat for dinner. I decided to go with eggs. I have made friends with the tabachi shop keeper. The grocery ladies are not friendly as of yet. I am still very tired and sleepy. Wish I could just stay put for 48 hours. My Italian Class in Firenze is getting better. It wasn't as hard today for some reason.

I think we should communicate via e-mail for a while; it seems you are better at not talking than me. But let's see. Write me back when you can. And thanks again for all of the wonderful things you sent me. I know I will enjoy all of them.

Peace.

Bill

Sub: Journey along
Date: 4/4/00 11:10:08 PM Eastern Daylight Time
From: NYCblackout
To: LEHUFF67

There's almost a foreign feeling of walking near a place you've never walked. Seeing something familiar. After a song and dance, all I'm thinking about is you. How two people can be one.

Really, I'm thinking about your name. How it sounds. A sweetness. It's a good feeling to hear you. Listen to you. Engage you.

At any moment, a warm feeling creeps up. A wild concoction. An odd formula etched on a piece of paper in Biology 206. Thrown in a chemical vat. Mixed up and tossed around.

Situated on a hill top between inductive and deductive. A fragile balance.

This is how it sounds as my heart, mind, and spirit circle each other. Occurring mostly when you're close. But they do a lot of grumbling, when you're away too. A rumbling when I sense your hopes, dangling above.

There's a certain ring, covering a big sensitive area. I'm not sure if I know why. I'm wondering aloud. Is it critical to arrive at an answer?

Until I pick up more of your signal,

Bill

Sub: «««.»»»
Date: 4/5/00 9:36:33 AM Eastern Daylight Time
From: NYCblackout
To: LEHUFF67

Again, why do you want to argue about something so simple? Complex, yes. Intricate, you bet. But just the basics. Minus the games. Such is the matter of your love for me.

Some French playwright said something on a wall in Paris. My memory on the name is fuzzy. I forget where the café is located (Left Bank or Right Bank). It's just somewhere in Paris.

> "Perfection isn't when you can't add nothing to it. Rather perfection is when you can't take anything from it."

This is how I'm feeling. This is what I feel. This is how I envision our love. It sits at a juncture. A certain point on the map of life—exactly where you can't take nothing from it. It stands alone. Strong and steady-like. Inspired primarily from above, our spirit and our dreams.

> What is it?
> How do you become worthy of love?
> How do you treasure a gift?
> How do you pay honor to honor?
> Cany you control giving?

I know of nothing to argue about.

May peace be with you, your family, and your love ones.

Bill

Sub: Unfolding
Date: 4/6/00 10:20:54 PM Eastern Daylight Time
From: NYCblackout
To: LEHUFF67

Really settling in on time schedules between London, Vienna and Cannes. Just realizing that these meetings need to a little better organized and coordinated.

One day you're outside. You sense something around the corner. Curiosity about an uncalled, perception. A wide boulevard, opening up a quaint vista, detailing all of what was missing before. Motivating a lateral sense. Dusting off your intuition. A deliberate sensitive. Very light and no glare. Seeping through tree leaves is a brightness from over yonder near destiny.

Alas, flowers blooming. A sudden breeze. A distinguishable chill- awakening sleep. Lately, a suspending mist prior to dawn. A smell of moisture, in the air. All signal a rumbling. A sweeping move. Silent upheaval followed by an interlude or intermezzo. Landing smack dab in the lap of discovery—a new walk.

Hoping your day was full. Really, I hope that peace was as close as the middle of your pillow, touching your cheek.

Bill

Sub: All right
Date: 4/7/0010:23:08 PM Eastern Daylight Time
From: NYCblackout
To: LEHUFF67

Sorry about all the confusion. Guess I was excited about hearing your voice in a long time. I kept running my mouth. I couldn't get the wax between my ears out of the way. Will you forgive me for being a hard head?

I was very excited that your friends recognized your dramatic inklings. That little touch, which makes your moves so special, so unique. You go, girl! Just got a call back from Kay's distributor contact. Ernest Smith got the package. He promised to expedite matters, get the delivery distribution contract. With that in place, we can finance the difference between $400,000 and $5,000,000. Screen Partners should then be able to fork up the difference. Now, it's beginning to feel fresh. Awesome.

I believe in you. I accept your words. I'm applauding your efforts. Every minute. Every hour. Throughout the day. As night comes and touches the moon. The task of taking it all in, is a long journey. Perhaps, it will take another life time. But I'm praying for an opportunity to join you.

I can feel your aura lingering. Not too far away. If anything, I'd like to be a partner on your escape. Once you clamp your foot, old man doubt has nowhere to go. I'm in love with you big time.

I'm hoping that peace remains near your eyes. Circling. In sight of sensation.

Sub: Aware
Date: 4/8/00 8:42:29 AM Eastern Daylight Time
From: NYCblackout
To: LEHUFF67@AOL.COM

It's early in the morning. I'm sorting through some crazy thoughts. Others would call it opening up to another reality. Maybe I'll jot these down for our story.

I'm aware of your love. It shakes me, like a jolt of lightening. I'm sensing an invisible urge. A heightened confidence. Your energy is present. Metamorphic over here, bearing essence. There are times when, my heart runs out of space, like it's all alone. Crashes into a vein of hope. Wandering off through an artery where it meets up with understanding. I'm waiting for you.

I hope your BBQ goes well. That all is good and prosperous with your day and night.

Peace,
Bill

Sub: (no subject)
Date: 4/9/00 8:40:02 AM Eastern Daylight Time
From: LEHUFF67
To: NYCblackout

Are you listening to me?

Sub: Listening...hearing...absorbing...U
Date: 4/9/00 6:20:57 PM Eastern Daylight Time
From: NYCblackout
To: LEHUFF67

So I'm into you completely. I'm for you, with no hesitation. I'm besides you. Behind you. Walking in front of you for shelter against alligators and wolves. I'm on board for the long haul. I'm really lucky to know you. I'm so fortunate to know about you. It's a blessing to recognize your powers.

Yet I'm lonely. But what makes me less lonely, is knowing you're over there. Knowing that you're working on your dream. Embracing our faith in the other. Accepting a deeper level of trust than I've ever known or experienced. Realizing what's happening is good. Even though it's tough.

Your nature continues to visit with me. Providing a unique kind of assurance.

I have love for you. I'm unsure of all of my emotions. However, I sense that they are growing. I know it's impossible to describe a feeling. Forming and shaping by its own volition. Yet I know that you're the only one that understands.

You're the (1).

Peace,
Bill

Sub: (no subject)
Date: 4/9/00 8:38:29 AM Eastern Daylight Time
From: LEHUFF67
To: NYCblackout

Excuse me. Can you get off the phone? I need to talk to you.

Sub: Repeat
Date: 4/9/00 4:05:36 PM Eastern Daylight Time
From: NYCblackout
To: LEHUFF67

Didn't know if this got sidetrack like the other piece. I wanted to send it again. Maybe, there was something I left off like usual.

I can't call it. It's way above me. I don't know what it is. Inconspicuously. It's inside. Wondering aimlessly. Everywhere I turn. It has the tone of an after ring. An odd silhouette at night.

It's a warm and fuzzy feeling that you're suspended, above us. Are you an angel? Divine creature? Accent eclectic? Do any of these equal unknown? Any of these dudes connected to knowing you? Are they why I'm drawn to your side?

Bill

Sub: Grazie
Date: 4/10/00 7:35:54 AM Eastern Daylight Time
From: NYCblackout
To: LEHUFF67

Grazie. Signorina LEONA

Quietly grateful, just leaving our creator. Embracing an attitude of nothing is impossible. Thankful for your love.

I'll be here for you. Whenever you want me. My love is nearby.

May peace complete its will with you.

Bill

Sub: Waiting
Date: 4/11/00 7:35:54 AM Eastern Daylight Time
From: NYCblackout
To: LEHUFF67

I'm becoming familiar with you. I've taken a liking to each petal, gently hanging from your blossom. Old man fear fades away. A soft nudge from your spirit. It is difficult resisting you.

While a renowned doctor injects a needle for curing a contagious disease, while an experienced nurse takes a temperature during a high fever—I have no immunity against your love. I have built no barriers against your consideration. I have no walls against your kindness from seeping in. No blockade against your touch. Wildness. I go by a different rhythm, when I see you.

We're moving to magnificence. Geography is irrelevant. Topography is not on the map. I'm closer to you. Your energy. You're aware of my thoughts—even while I'm shaking.

Still waiting for an answer. An Angel? Divine creature? Ancient eclectic? A holy ghost? All of the above? At the moment, I want to pat you on the head. Until I pick up more of your signals, my meditation is on peace.

Bill

Sub: Over Yonder
Date: 4/12/00 9:35:02 AM Eastern Daylight Time
From: NYCblackout
To: LEHUFF67

Physically, it hasn't happened. Living in the material world, I haven't gone there.

As a small child
A Bible phrase
Heaven and Hell
Purgatory

But since I meet you, I've detected a different state of mind. New meaning.

Ebbing river
Absence of conflict
Missing arrows
Unsuspecting turns
Unfolding flowers
Sprouting
Blending
Passing lightness
Anticipation

It's a wild feeling. Uniting what was separate. I felt it this morning when you called. When you were silent. During the time we talked. Discovering each other again. I felt it especially, when I called you back to talk about nature. I'm feeling not too far away from Heaven with you. There's nothing to say when we're over yonder.

An unseen wonder signals upward. Getting acquainted, with infinite hilltops. If our Creator sees fit to, grant me another day of life. I hope to tell you things that I couldn't utter before.

Until I hear more of your signals, I'm meditating that peace continues to be your all your buddy. Your best friend. Do take care of your throat. Tea. Water. Rest and more rest.

Later

Forbearing

Sub: (no subject)
Date: 4/14/00 12:05:17 PM Eastern Daylight Time
From: LEHUFF67
To: NYCblackout

Bill,

I can offer no defense for my actions. I admit total responsibility for treating you in an unkind, unloving manner. There is no question. I was and am wrong. I violated you and your friendship.

I have conflicting, mixed, earth-shattering emotions about you. About our relationship, about what it means. About where it is going. About where it has been.

Clearly, I depend on you for so much, perhaps too much. I care about you. I love you. You have given me so very much, more than I can say. More than I know how to say. More than I have ever known before.

I get crazy when it becomes clear, more so than not that our relationship is. What is it? I don't want an intimate relationship. But to say we have not one is rather silly. You know my deepest thoughts, just as you have shared yours with me. Intimacy.

What I should say what I want to say. It seems, I had said before, but I get scared. I get confused.

I get remarkable unable to handle the fact that we have crossed the line between what's physical and not, I wonder. I think I have said it before. It will be difficult for me to not have you in my life, but it is better that you are not made to suffer with my weaknesses and character flaws. Really, this won't go away.

Surely, you can find another person to share all your love. I am not worthy of your gifts. I am blocking your way. Your path. Your destiny.

Go now without me. I will only bring you unhappiness and regret. You deserve much more and much better.

Lee

Sub: lllll/Illlllll
Date: 4/16/00 1:22:28 AM Eastern Daylight Time
From: NYCblackout
To: LEHUFF67

I hear you. However, the gravity of the moment says something else is happening, beyond a word. A brief morning telephone conversation. A silence, here and there.

An empty feeling surrounds me.

I'm still confused. Wondering if everything will be all right. I went to the laundry without any washing powder. I drove around the city and almost had a couple of wrecks. Half the time, I didn't know where I was. Next, I went to install a computer system. To pass the time, I started talking about cross word puzzles to the client. All of a sudden, I had to excuse myself to the bathroom, just to cry.

Today and tonight, things have been very heavy. Instead of that light feathery feeling when you're nearby. I was afraid. Confused. Things started to change, when my thoughts wandered over to the small opening, in front of K-Mart. It felt just like when we first meet. You're were so close, circling around where we stood. I started believing again that things were ok.

Right now, I'm crying from a thought of you being alive, you being who you are. You experiencing mounds of happiness. Elevating within a wide space, between your heart, soul, and spirit.

There's not a phase of time that I don't consider how much you mean to me. How I yearn to touch your aura. See you smiling. Hear you talk to me. Down deep, I have a small feeling that everything will be all right for you and for what you're doing. Of course, this occurs without any assistance.

So within two weeks, I hope to write to you again. Maybe, a silent prayer is answered. A revelation of sorts. A shared understanding. There's some kind of magic about you. Exclusive of any battle or fight. A better understanding. So until it's all right. My hope is peace flying beside with you and all the folks you love so much.

Bill

Sub: LONG ENDURING
Date: 4/16/00 4:46:46 PM Eastern Daylight Time
From: NYCblackout
To: LEHUFF67

Mass inclination
Eloquent few
Plenty mellow
Anew floating
Discovery tracing
Surging
Second exposure

Thanks for the wake-up call. You're good at that.

I continue to learn from you. What's up with that? I'm also learning that competition is against US. So I'm more aware of where we are. Where we can go. Where we could go. Please rest up. Feel out your dreams. Maybe a local grocery store.

Please continue to share space with consideration.

Love,
Bill

Sub: (no subject)
Date: 4/17/00 6:26:51 AM Eastern Daylight Time
From: LEHUFF67
To: NYCblackout

Hey,

I changed my mind. Call me.

Lee

Sub: Fwd:
Date: 4/17/00 6:46:25 AM Eastern Daylight Time
From: LEHUFF67
To: NYCblackout

Martin,

You poor baby. I'm so sad that you are sad. There is nothing like heartache. And the COG has yet to pop out a pill for it, so all you can do is weather the storm. I know it hurts way down deep. All the way to the bottom of your soul. I know it's hard, but try and remember Jay is not all there. His is without a conscience. Just think about that for a while.

I know it doesn't help so much, when you consider all of the time and words that have passed between you. But really, you know he is not real. He is not a real, total person. I know you may think of words and actions of his, and go back and forth. I know, I know, I know. Look, if you send his stuff back, please consider sending it COD, Ok?

Three years is a long time to forget. And the unresolved nature of the situation I know is making you crazy. I am no psychiatrist, but would that help? Being able to throw him up against the wall, spit on him, kick him, and get it out, if only for you? I am not trying to instigate. I am just wondering if that might help. Maybe some anger therapy, you know beating up a pillow or something?

You know that one day this will be behind you, and, yes, you will be happy again. You will be.

Is Joy still eating a bag of candy a day?

Last night, I went to the laundry mat. Needed to dry my clothes.

So because I am American and have been exposed to advertising,

I think as make my way to the laundry mat, about that commercial. You know the one, where the two meet and blah, blah, blah. So I get there, and of course, nothing but lose fitting jeans wearing hair-dyed Americans and their respective stereotypical classmates. Ok. No big surprise. No big letdown.

I am still in the wash mode. And in walks Mister all-American. He is from a good family. He has beautiful skin, teeth, hair, eyes, education, wit, and personality. He walks right up to me and begins to inquire about the system. So I think he is just in need of information. He sits down next to me and starts spinning tales of being in Africa, helping at a hospital Good Samaritan. I am completely mesmerized. He is playing me up, flirting, pulling out all the stops. Offering to help me fold my sheets, looking to see if I'm wearing a wedding ring. The whole 9 yards. I am so enraptured by him that I let my dry clothes sit in the dryer, so as not to miss a word he utters.

Our clothes finished. He asks me to go to the Internet cafe. I go as we are folding, I said, "I am not completely dry. Are you?"

Mr. Wonderful says, "No. "Wherever I sleep tonight, I will put these out to dry."

I respond with, "What do you mean?"

He looks up from the clothes pile and spits out, "Oh, I am going to Geneva tonight on the 10:50 train." Then he says, "I have to go back to the hotel and pack, do you want to walk with me?"

Ok. On the way to his hotel, mind you, all the while, he is, "you walk on the side walk," "do you want me to carry your bags?" (I had two big shopping bags of clothes) and on and on. I am envisioning children, Christmas. Martin, he was so it. He was beyond it.

We were walking and he says, "So you want to go to Geneva with me?" To which, I say nothing, because, because, because. We go to his hotel, four floors up, he says, "Do you want me to carry your bags?" It is four floors. He packs. I watch. Oh, it is now 50 minutes until the train departs. Sorry.

We are back on the street, walking to the station, where I had parked. He says again, "So do you want to go to Geneva with me?"

I look at him and say, "And then what?"

"Whatever your heart desires." Hello! Am I in? Is this real?

He says, "The train leaves in 50 minutes, which means, you don't have enough time to go home and pack. You have clean clothes, and I think I saw some underwear."

Of course, my head is spinning. Of course, I am considering the possibility. Oh my god! Is this real or what ? I look at him and say, "Go to Geneva, with two shopping bags?" It's not that I wouldn't like to go, and that I wouldn't enjoy the company, but it's just not practical.

We are approaching the station, and I tell him I am writing a story. He replies, "Fiction?" Yes. "Does it have substance?" I think he is asking if I have substance. I come back with, "I shouldn't have to answer that question."

He says, "No. You don't have to answer any questions I ask." Then the whole thing falls apart. "That's the great thing about traveling. You can meet people and tell them anything. It does not matter. You can say whatever you want." And then the bubble burst. And I was horrified. He was not real. After all, he was make-believe. Boy oh boy, I will never forget him. Ever.

So that happened.

I have finished Italian lessons. I called the whole thing off. I went to the director of the school and asked for help and/or a refund. He gave a stupid solution aimed at keeping my money. MF!

I went to the Beauty Parlor of Florence today. And the old, head honcho, hairdresser man did my hair. I was so afraid, but he did a great job. All the other clients were old, roll my hair, set, and perm ladies. It was an experience. Oh, and I smoked a cigarette, while the color set in!

Life isn't all that bad, even if I can't speak the language! Keep your chin up. That's the only way to see the sun and let it shine on your face! Good luck with the installs.

Lee

Sub: Excellent
Date: 4/17/00 11:21:42 AM Eastern Daylight Time
From: NYCblackout
To: LEHUFF67

The more I learn, the more I want to learn about you.

You're contagious. Your love is spreading like a wild desert fire. Sharing warmth right under. A special spot. Only two can detect, at once.

You're an old soul. Crafted through early imagination. Nobody in their right mind ever took time, to read it. Even at the end of a daytime nightmare, they conceived of it as only a book.

Sprouting from your heart.
Sharing a page.
Another page.
No questions.
Each page
Fragility
Every verb
Different sensation
Brave pronunciation
Soothing vibration
Each nuance
Softness
Each revelation
Unrelenting
Imagination
Creation
Magic—at once

Every chapter reveals more and more of what was missing. I'm struggling to get out of the way...

Your willingness to open a small, tiny crack. Between a sensitive impulse. A soaring energy. Protecting your most intricate reservations.

Could you give some thought to writing a story with me? We could share energy beyond a physical being? Suspended somewhere beyond where we stand. It could be anything we understand or don't understand. Any idea that scares us or some feeling unfamiliar to our hearts. Could this be a concept?

Hidden Faces—a story that tracks a struggling American writer. He's up and down South France and Northern Italian Coast. He endears himself with the Vienna's parks and music. His high is Turkish coffee. He's downright happy with the beers from Northwest Germany. One day in Florence, he spots an exotic photojournalist. Their budding relationship examines old prejudices not only about humans but about Europe. Really, does an artist have to leave home to become full or accepted by the masses? Why did Picasso leave Spain for France? What's up with Rilke going back and forth? Do we get to discover another side of ourselves, when we travel? Does a stranger change our perceptions? What does color have to do with anything?

We're experimenting
Making a mess
Cracking eggs
Following an escape
Crafting
Enduring silence
Working a fear
Chiseling time
Sculpting rocks
Outside boundaries

Floating flutter by
Flying free
Releasing will

And as usual, you're right. I got to get to work. Airline ticket. My negotiating hat. Coordinating between Wolfgang & Martin. Blending mind-sets. Pulling out the old ego. Eliminating old nemesis—the dream killer. It's time to get out of Dodge City!

If God ever allowed you to become sick or get a broken bone or whatever, I want to be there for you. I'd want to hold your hand. Pull your head up, against a pillow. That way, you'd be comfortable enough to slip into quiet. Rub a damp cloth along your forehead to remove any fever sweat. I'd want to pamper you or bring you a big old chocolate chip cookie.

Ciao.

Bill

Sub: (no subject)
Date: 4/18/00 7:16:34 AM Eastern Daylight Time
From: LEHUFF67
To: NYCblackout

Thank you for the talk this morning.

You have brought me back to life. Back to myself. I am feeling better. More in touch with mostly everything. How blessed I am to have someone who can and does appreciate who I am, and who can remind me. You don't get half as much cheerleading from me, though it seems. Why do you stay around?

Why do you fight my suggestions, at times? Perhaps, now you can hear me better or will choose to listen. Your choice, right? Well, I think we've been here once or twice before. I guess I have to learn to accept it. I will never understand why it has to take so long to get a movie made. Why can't you change that? Why accept things the way they are? Other business happens faster, why can't this? You got an answer for that? Give it to me. The short version.

What are you doing?

Lee

Sub: Happy
Date: 4/18/00 11 :05:35 PM Eastern Daylight Time
From: NYCblackout
To: LEHUFF67

Just a thought. I'm so happy knowing you're getting thru all the old jive. I'm happy too that you're with me. Your words from yesterday, still linger. Seems like you're here now. Everything is straight. All right.

Thank you, for standing by me, during a hectic morning. A weird AM and into the night. Thanks for nudging that little kick in the butt. You were with me. You were beside me. You were there, for me.

Until I hear more of your signals, my love remains with you.

Bill

Sub: Re: Lodging
Date: 4/19/00 7'37: 37 PM Eastern Daylight Time
From: LEHUFF67
To: NYCblackout

What happened?
Why do I feel screwed?
And so how was it for you?

Lee

Sub: (no subject)
Date: 4/21/00 4:30:19 PM Eastern Daylight Time
From: LEHUFF67
To: NYCblackout

Hey!
Call me before you go to sleep!

Quiet Rumbling

Sub: Quietly
Date: 4/21/00 6:45:15 PM Eastern Daylight Time
From: NYCblackout
To: LEHUFF67

Is this how we come to each other? Arriving without pretense. No agenda. Sharing hopes to be near one another—only if it's right.

My love for you refuses to run away.

Bill

Sub: TODAY
Date: 4/22/00 7:18:12 AM Eastern Daylight Time
From: NYCblackout
To: LEHUFF67

I'm hoping your day is quiet. Peaceful. Cool.

Last night. Rest was dreamlike. Solemn. Long.

I found myself in the cradle of your arms. Quietly, as you slept.

I'll be @ Office Depot Sandy Springs 404-257--0123 until 21:30 hr. or thereabouts.

Peace,
Bill

Sub: Burning slowly
Date: 4/23/00 9:11: 11 AM Eastern Daylight Time
From: NYCblackout
To: LEHUFF67

Your high spirit roams about. Over here. I'm bumping into you. I'm wishing your morning, day, and night are full of good hopes.

A little before somewhere between 3:30 / 4:00 AM (9:30 / 10:00 AM) your time. I got up, thinking deeply about what you were doing. I knelt down to say a prayer for you. Through no direction of my own, I'm aware of some notions, which were hollered out.

That your day was full. Your health improves. Maybe the exact amount of minerals, vitamins, nutrients be contained in the veggies you picked up yesterday. That the water you drink is sufficient. That your spirit flows freely. That you have the power to remove yourself, from friction. Outside from resistance. Reduce static from your movements. That your love floats freely. Landing upon any spot. Destination you see fit. That the Creator's will somehow links up to your will. Done.

Then I grabbed some incense. I placed it on your table area. Your mantle, near the door. It was prominent right smack dab in the front, middle of the table. Then I lighted incense and a candle. Something inside plopped me down on the couch, just in time to catch a full scene. It was vibrant radiant flame, burning softly and bright. It refused to waver back and forth. There are some words you just can't abbreviate. Perfect is one of them.

I have much love for you. It filters, radiates, close to this strong, brilliant flame I'm watching from across the room.

It's all right. Everything's going to all right bye and bye.

Peace,
Bill

Sub: Ever brightly
Date: 4/24/00 1:55:00 AM Eastern Daylight Time
From: NYCblackout
To: LEHUFF67

After so many lumps and bumps. Time hassles (from 3:30 AM until the next morning). Your candle. Still burns lightly.

No longer
Hassle
Bother
Embracing
Silence
Understanding
Perception
Awareness
Uninterrupted
Constantly
Allowing
Solitude

I'm thinking about how your happiness. I'm longing to see your face. Sparkles in your eyes. Your fingers rubbing freshly cut flowers. Every time I smell a pink rose, I can feel you.

Every day I'm learning to accept more of our love. As time unfolds, I'm opening up to what it was before we meet. My arms are open to our future.

Until I hear more of your signal, peace be with you.

Bill

Sub: ????
Date: 4/24/00 10:08:32 AM Eastern Daylight Time
From: NYCblackout
To: LEHUFF67

Are you back on the block? Are you tearing things up? Did your rest come around? Have you started moving and shaking things up? Are you feeling yourself again? Where're you? Any dirt flying yet?

Really, I miss you. 1 miss your laugh. Your smile. Those bright rays, coming from you. When you grin. When you're loose. When you let go. Particularly, when you're on the ground.

Peace is with you.

Bill

Sub: A fresh vision
Date: 4/25/00 9:55:40 AM Eastern Daylight Time
From: NYCblackout
To: LEHUFF67

OK. Once you left him. You went over there before. Looking for love (like in the letter you wrote). Your dream come true. A set back or two. Then you come back home…

Off you go again, looking for roots. A history to reacquaint and to find a connection that you lost. Take a picture. Capture the scene. It's this ancient feeling. I'm behind you on all of your energy. Moving forward. You experience a few hiccups. You're disappointed in the scene. You're taken off your feet and dropped again. I'm with you all the time.

What made me mad this morning? Why go back? You're moving forward. What's up with this crap about loyalty from Americans? Why are you giving that any power? Why do you dilute your essence with small talk? This lady Suzanne not talking to you? Not having the time of day for you? Some Turkish guy talking about loyalty? What's up with the distractions?

Your experiences shape your reality. Or when you forget, your reality can shape your experience. You have this choice, all the time. Mr. preacher doesn't necessarily want to talk directly to the senior choir, because he knows where they're coming from. Occasionally, he may holler out, "Can I get an Amen?" Other times, he may shout out, "Can I get a witness?" The deacon board doesn't necessarily want to shout to the usher board, because they know where they're coming from.

Your aura is signaling a baby's nature. An injured bird—your ruffled feathers remain a sight of beauty. Your wings are swollen, from the weight of the world's hang-ups. As somebody use to flights of fancy, you're anxious to take off. You're chopping at the bit to do some serious roaming. On your path over to where you're going is a trip not many have taken.

Your arrival is not one for, many words. It's not subject to discussion. It's not a matter of opinion. Only a feeling due you linked to your essence. I just happen to love you more than words. It's a love which follows your every step. Praying for your flight, while you're flying—as you land over yonder.

So I am not mad at you. I love you very mucho. Sleep well. Peace.

Bill

Sub: ++++++++++
Date: 4/29/00 9:54:13 AM Eastern Daylight Time
From: NYCblackout
To: LEHUFF67

Just admiring a shining heart from afar. Constantly, I'm wishing that goodness travel near you. A happy feeling encircles you, all the time.

Peace

Bill

Sub: +++====!
Date: 5/1/00 3:23:20 PM Eastern Daylight Time
From: NYCblackout
To: LEHUFF67

Did you have a peaceful drive thru the Italian countryside? Did the birds visit you? I felt your grin.

I'm missing you.

Peace,
Bill

Sub: GRAZIE
Date: 5/2/00 2:51:25 AM Eastern Daylight Time
From: NYCblackout
To: LEHUFF67

Thanks for this morning. Every hour. Each day. More and more. I'm appreciating your essence.

Peace,
Bill

Sub: El Progresso
Date: 5/2/00 2:24:25 AM Eastern Daylight Time
From: NYCblackout
To: LEHUFF67

I took more pictures of Booby with Maria. Tonight when I got home. The tall Russian asked when you were coming home. I said, "In about four weeks."

Next up, I headed over to Thomas's pad to load software. Another wall. I have to pick up a serial converter tomorrow @ work to complete the connection. Sometime this week, you should have pictures of Booby. I'm leaning toward Kim Basinger as Roselyn Jones—a vision of quaintness, down home nature, animal rights, environmental proximity, togetherness all linking an essence to *Sugar & Spice*.

In the morning and Thursday (my day off), I'll contact her agent. She is from Georgia. She's not up to Hollywood jive. She lives on Long Island, a country bumpkin in the Big Apple. So we'll see where this leads us. Maybe it could be a backup situation to Paris. Kim makes financing more realistic, due to her star appeal. It would be interesting how you and her would hit it off.

I'm missing you a lot. I'm yearning for your smile's glow. Just a brief second, to look in your eyes and be closer to you. Until I pick up more of your signals.

Peace,
Bill

Sub: Movements
Date: 5/4/00 4:20:24 AM Eastern Daylight Time
From: NYCblackout
To: LEHUFF67

I'm with your every step. Even through all of the shuffling and ups and downs.

A word from a fortune cookie:

> "Your present plans are going to succeed".

I hope your sleep was quite. Solemn. I miss your touch. Your little smile. Still, I'm waiting for you—for our time.

Peace,
Bill

Sub: Acting Services—'Sugar & Spice'
Date: 5/6/00 2:30:24 AM Eastern Daylight Time
From: NYCblackout
To: LEHUFF67

Hope all is well with you. Your family. Your unfolding. I miss hearing your voice. Your quirks. Where are you now? What're you doing (2:22 AM–8:22 AM coast time)?

Attached is an offer regarding the story. Until I hear your signals. Nearby.

Peace,
Bill

Sub: Incognito
Date: 5/7/00 5:21 :07 AM Eastern Daylight Time
From: NYCblackout
To: LEHUFF67

How come you lose your mind with me? Drag your feet? Throwing me a cold shoulder. An indifferent shrug? A sly ciao?

I'm hoping that your sleep returns to calm. This intimate and warm thought of you woke me up. I felt you—your journey. How are you? Really, I'm wishing you courage, strength and warm energy. Actually, I've been thinking about you more than a wild imagination. I've been missing a unique vibration from you.

Until I hear your signal.

Peace,
Bill

Sub: ********
Date: 5/8/00 10:27:37 PM Eastern Daylight Time
From: NYCblackout
To: LEHUFF67

What's with the "Italian funk?"

Is it any consolation to remember who you were, before you arrived over there? Does it ring any comfort to know that you were good, approaching excellence, before you stepped off the plane in Rome?

Just because folks want to step on you, does that really mean you want to step on them too? What's the deal on continuing to question your own motives? Pointing fingers at yourself? Can you take a pause? A time-out? A recess and have some fun with yourself. What does it feel like to have some playtime with your ideas? Maybe some folly with your dreams?

Again, what have they done, in the course of life, to hurt or derail you, as much as you've allowed? Do they actually deserve as much power as you've handed over to them? What's up with that? Sometime last week, you sounded like you were back on the block. What happened?

I'm hoping that you're all right. I'm hoping you're safe inside. I'm wishing that your happiness glows, in a warm direction. I'm thinking that your intuition is connected to your family's own design of what you want or your hopes. Meditation lingers on your solace, quiet time, and instincts, for what you want to do.

For sure, I wish peace continues to dwell nearby.

Bill

Sub: + more
Date: 5/9/00 4:30:41 AM Eastern Daylight Time
From: NYCblackout
To: LEHUFF67

Yeah.

When you think about it, you've got too much going on to let anything or anyone stop you.

I'm hoping that you're happier. I love you more everyday—more than ever before.

Peace,
Bill

Sub: All the more
Date: 5/11/00 11:27:11 PM Eastern Daylight Time
From: NYCblackout
To: LEHUFF67

Our talks today. Again today. And tonight opened me up again to your warm probing glow. Your warm radiance.

Really, it's a solid feeling to know you're in my life. That we're learning about each other. We listen. We hear a similar note, from a gothic symphony. Harboring close, to an unfolding familiar pulse.

You're all over my mind. Tossing and turning. A little later on a stretch from around my pillow. Then I'm feeling everything is all right with you.

Please be careful on this trip. Near the water. Until I hear more of your signals. I'm hoping peace remains your best friend. High above, double-talk, and jive. I'm with you.

Ciao.

Bill

Nearby Landing

Sub: Feet on the ground - Hotel Mas Djoliba
Date: 5/17/00 5:03:41 AM Eastern Daylight Time
From: NYCblackout
To: LEHUFF67

When I got off the plane in Nice, I took the next train to Antibes. I had no idea of where I wanted to stay or to meet you. This notion of idealistic was festering, but I couldn't put my finger on anything.

I watched as the train came to a slow stop at the Antibes Platform (a rail line surrounded by a small station and nearby water). I saw some cabbies near the entrance and a rack of pamphlets. I grabbed one and flipped through it. I saw this description of a rustic building. I asked the cabbie who luckily spoke English, and he said that it was called Mas Djoliba Hotel. He said it was walking distance from the ocean. Right away I said, "Take me there!"

Here's the address:

29, avenue de Provence
06600 ANTIBES
(33) 04 93 34 02 48 Tel
(33) 04 93 34 05 81 Fax

It only took me a few minutes to center on the Gardens at Mas Djoliba. They are beyond description. Your eyes are drawn to lilacs. Eucalyptus. Daisies. Roses. Water lilies. Subtle arrangements of native shrubs. Intricate trees. The flower's aroma follows you to the lobby. As you sit around a small lobby area, you'll hear the shoveling sound of a gardner. This alerts you out to watch a butterfly, extracting nutrients.

Can you make time for Antibes?

Bill

Sub: Provence Country Side
Date: 5/19/00 7:49:30 PM Eastern Daylight Time
From: NYCblackout
To: LEHUFF67

My rental car was a trip. I got excited from the sound of our car's receding exhaust, as we were circling the "roundabout" near Antibes. It was though we were old hands. It was almost like we had lived in the place, all the time.

The French country side is so cool. The mountains. Steep valleys. Sharp curves, blending into mountains as I rode the clutch. Listening to radio music and singing a line or two together. However, the best part of getting lost was rolling into the parking lot of a country house that turned out to be Pinocchio's. Soft crust French bread. Gruyere Cheese. Off the scale local red wines.

We could argue about Aix and those exquisite red wines. Outstanding. I felt a new level with you, when we stopped for a potty break at the road side gas station. It was so normal but so unordinary. I felt terribly closer to you.

About tonight's meal:

Sylvain has elaborated a summer menu from local fresh local products. The diner needs special preparation and must be served at a precise moment. In order to appreciate all the flavor of this meal (our priority is your satisfaction), we give you a rendezvous at 19h30, and not later please.

Bon Appétit.

I miss you.

Bill

Sub: Antibes
Date: 5/24/00 7:49:30 PM Eastern Daylight Time
From: NYCblackout
To: LEHUFF67

The German couple from Wiesbaden, Germany had some thought about you as you left. They were eating breakfast & dinner behind you on Sunday.

They thought you were from Scandinavia (have you heard that one, before?).

The wife thought that you were my muse.

The guy said, "Tell your muse, we said hello."

I couldn't agree with them more.

Peace.

Sub: Forgiving
Date: 5/25/00 6:50:55 AM Eastern Daylight Time
From: NYCblackout
To: LEHUFF67

Leona,

During a fortnight (or these past three days/nights), I've been lost. Uneasy. Uptight. Uncomfortable. Because of some ancient fear, I doubted your word. My words from Monday night expressed disbelief in your words, your character, your essence.

On Monday night, my words missed the boat. On Monday night, I did not acknowledge you. Miserably, honor was missing. I wasn't thinking.

Our argument or blow up on Monday started over some "jive-time" story. ricky - tack stuff. It went like - who was the real wine expert? Which one of us had a chalet in the Rhine Valley and had grown award-winning grapes? What is bouquet? Did any of these questions really matter? We were just two Americans, sitting in dump of a restaurant, wanting a glass of good wine to go with our pasta. Are you going to let an argument over wine stop our relationship? What is most important—materiality or love?

Can you forgive me? Can you help me understand a mistake? Is there forbearance on not thinking? I need your patience on me working through a setback. Is it possible to lift the barbed wire fence? It is painful to be near you, yet so far away.

My heart stings. Only you know what to do. I can't say so much. Not so much about my love. Right now, I'm feeling more love for you.

Bill

Sub: Re: Forgiving
Date: 5/25/004:19:34 PM Eastern Daylight Time
From: LEHUFF67
To: NYCblackout

I am in no way looking for, needing, wanting.

Allowing myself to be put down? Told I am wrong, weak, or worthless. I have no time for any such thing. I am far too old to put up with crap like that. I have already lived that chapter. I went to therapy, even though you have no respect for the fact that I work on my emotional issues in therapy, because of it, am aware. So, later for you!!! fuck you.

Another example of my weakness? Those are your thoughts and feelings. Whether you are right or wrong, it matters not. These things belong to you. And please keep them all to yourself. Or share them with some other incomplete idiot willing to take it and listen to it. I am out the door. *Finito.*

Forgive you? Forgive you for what you feel and think of me? Yeah. OK. I can't quite make sense of it. That should not surprise you at all. Right? I seek to burden you no longer with my shortcomings, my less than self. My second rate existence. My inability to do anything without fucking screwing it up.

I have considered a restraining order. I have wondered what else you might do to me. With my name, with my letters. I am quite certain you would get sued if you published them without my consent. Is that what you want?

Leave me alone.

Lee

Sub: Hoping
Date: 5/30/00 11:04:18 AM Eastern Daylight Time
From: NYCblackout
To: LEHUFF67

An eerie silence. Circling everything. I'm sad. I've been crying. I've missed your voice. You're doing your thing. All of a sudden, you discover something else. You frame a little child's smile. Coming across something for the first time. During a solitary walk home, from school.

I'm no longer surprised by the silence…I'm waiting for something to come out of the distance. Over the horizon. Could you return? Soothe things over.

I love you now. I love you tomorrow. Each minute joins an hour. An hour meets day. Light crosses darkness.

Peace,
Bill

Sub: Grateful
Date: 6/01/ 00 10:06:16 PM Eastern Daylight Time
From: NYCblackout
To: LEHUFF67

I'm feeling thankful for your visit with me. It's a feeling I've longed to know. Again. I hope to visit with you soon.

I don't have to travel too far to touch a gold mine. Close to my heart. Your love lives on top of me. Beside me. Your love is quiet warm. I want you here. 1 want to see you. All I want is good to happen.

Until I hear from you, I'm hoping peace continues to be with you.

Bill

Sub: Patience
Date: 6/6/00 9:43:54 AM Eastern Daylight Time
From: NYCblackout
To: LEHUFF67

I'm waiting for you. Waiting for healing. Waiting for solitude. Waiting for silence. Down deep, I know this can only happen when things are right.

I want you to be happy. Surely now, you're aware that I'm one of your cheerleaders. Somebody on the sidelines. Far away. Rooting for your success. Hoping. Wishing. Blossoming dreams. Anew reality. Full confidence. Unfolding.

I'm with you.

Bill

Sub: (no subject)
Date: 6/10/00 6:26:59 PM Eastern Daylight Time
From: LEHUFF67
To: NYCblackout

Get off line.

Lee

Afterthoughts

Sub: “Sugar & Spice”
Date: 6/10/006:05:44 PM Eastern Daylight Time
From: NYCblackout
To: eric.aron@infonie. fr

Eric,

Thanks for your prompt e-mail. I’m excited about learning and sharing with you. OK. Today, I mailed you a full version of the script and attachments. I felt that e-mailing would take away the story’s “gesso.” The script program is a DOS-based program so I wasn’t sure if it would come out clear to you. Anyway, by express postal, it should be to you within 4/5 days.

Just recently, when I was in Antibes, near Cannes for the film festival and to meet with Screen Partners. In London, I met my girl friend in Antibes. Our hotel was beyond majestic. Almost near magical for its structure and solace. It was an impression of silence. Mixed with an enlightening sea breeze, shining light from a harbor house along with early morning bird chirping. Peace was floating in every breeze.

Then we went to a restaurant that we weren’t even suppose to go. I got lost in Nice, and it was something we just dropped by. It was much different that our experience at Pinochio’s. A stupid argument over wine, and what wine did or did not do. I was taken out of nature. Next thing you know - I was drifting between different alley spaces in Old Antibes. Desperately trying and hoping to find something to take me away from the pain. Away from the madness of being rejected. That dark notion of being alone and being lost, at once.

Then I went into an alleyway. I saw a couple sitting down at a table. They were eating pastry and sharing it with their little baby. That whole scene was quite humbling and solemn. Then this music made its way through the air, from a music shop. I followed the vibe over to the store and discovered it was "India," your CD. The same guy from outside (eating with the baby) came in and greeted me as monsieur. Respectful. I asked about the music, and he told me it was Eric Aron, a composer who travelled to different countries and made music, based on his understanding of the culture. I thought that was pretty awesome. I would like to learn more about your understanding about an image, just in front of our eyes.

Right now, I'm listening to "Himalaya." Indeed, could you forward a copy of your resume or musical activities? This will be part of our financing package to allow Screen Partners, who will be composing/recording music. I would like to meet with you, sometime in early fall (September/October), when I'm in Paris. If you will be in country, please let me know a place/time convenient for you. I hope you have a good read. I am curious on your impressions of the story. If you should have any questions and/or comments, feel free to e-mail or call me @ (770) 394-7584.

Until I hear from you, you have my warm regards.

Bill

Sub: Souvenirs d'Antibes
Date: 6/12/00 12:41:17 PM Eastern Daylight Time
From: WernerFreund@t-online.de (Werner Freund)
To: NYCblackout@AOL.com

Hello Bill,

I regret to have you waiting for a message so long after we heard from you before the end of May, even though we have remembered you quite often.

We are grateful for having had you with us that night at Antibes. I am afraid I have probably grasped only a smaller part of what moved you at that time; I feel like having had a glimpse of a world I am not at all familiar with. I feel a bit richer now that I had the opportunity of talking to you through that evening.

Mirja's and my concern has been whether the hopes and expectations by which you were being borne at that time were sufficiently corroborated by factual circumstances to make it possible for you to transform at least part of these expectations into life. We very much do hope so, and our best wishes are with you!

During Thursday and Friday of that week, I attended a conference on new technologies and e-commerce in the financial business and related topics; it was quite good. The following Saturday, we spent driving through the French Rivera's back mountains, visiting an oil mill and a vineyard in order to replenish our respective stocks.

Coming back toward Antibes, we drove along the coast west of Cannes and saw a landscape quite different from the one around Antibes and Cannes, where reddish rocks stretch right into the sea. Very impressive, particularly so in the light of the setting sun! Well and on Sunday, we drove up the Rhone valley, through the French Jura Mountains, and then up the Rhine valley back to Wiesbaden. Despite some bad whether, we got home safe.

Now everyday life has us again—I am back at my project with Deutsch Bank, and Mirja has just started on a new project with a distributor of computer network components, conceiving and organizing a large event to take place in October at Frankfurt. (It is her first project as a freelancer after she gave up her employment a year ago.)

Still we trust we shall find some weeks during the summer to spend at our holiday place in southwest Finland. If ever you be in the Rhine-Main area, do come and see us! In the meantime, let us stay in touch!

My best regards (and Mirja insists on my extending hers as well) to you and to Leona!

Werner

PS 1:

Is traffic really the main topic in Atlanta?

PPS:

There is some film producing companies in Wiesbaden. Please look up at http:www.taunusfilm.coml.

Werner Freund
Im Rosenfeld 8 D-65203 Wiesbaden
telephone +49-700-AmicCons (+49-700-26422667)
mobile +49-170-5560025
telecopy +49-611-601508
e-mail Werner. Freund@AmicConsult.com

Sub: Garden
Date: 6/13/00 9:52:46 AM Eastern Daylight Time
From: NYCblackout
To: LEHUFF67

I feel richer from having seen you on Sunday.

I get a steady feeling from plants. The garden at Mas Djoliba. It was a crazy connection when I gave you the bouquet of flowers from Cannes Flower Market. I can't describe your expression. Your smile reflected a bunch of green. You feel like a garden.

Space
Acres
Clarity
Sustenance
No scarecrows
Each greenery
Each fragrance
Shedding beauty
Easy growth
Dirt mounds
Strong roots
Wild grass
Varietal blooms
Colorful leaves
Winding branches
Aroma
Uniting
Old = new
Heavy = inconsequential
Dark = bright day

Visiting your garden. Makes me aware. Who I am.

Peace,
Bill

Sub: Acting Services -"Sugar & Spice"
Date: 6/23/00 11:47:41 PM Eastern Daylight Time
From: NYCblackout
To: LEHUFF67
File: leona.rtf (10943 bytes)
DL Time (26400 bps): < 1 minute

Hola,

Attached is a revised offer. I'd be interested in your questions and thoughts.

Congratulations on your writing. Things are shaping up for you. I'm behind you. Along every step. Then too, I'm with you.

Until I hear from you.

Peace,
Bill

Sub: (no subject)
Date: 6/25/00 11:58: 13 AM Eastern Day light Time
From: LEHUFF67
To: NYCblackout

Looking for article.

Lee

Appendix

Sub: Organic Wraps
Date: 9/29/2005 9:20:25 AM. Eastern Daylight Time
From: jkliot@oQencit films.com
To: NYCblackout@aol.com

I run HDNet Films. Do you have a script for your project?

Jason

Sub: Re: Organic Wraps
Date: 9/29/2005 5:50:50 P.M. Eastern Daylight Time
From: NYCblackout
To: jkliot@opencityfilms.com

Yes.

I can send the script and preliminary production estimate on Tuesday, October 4, 2005. Is there a specific address I should it send it to?

Thanks,
Bill

CITY FOOD

Insignia: Signature Cuisine

BILL SWEENEY

Insignia<in-, in + signum ... a mark, a badge, emblem or other distinguishing mark ... a letter or number on the 1st page...
—*Webster's Dictionary*

Inside Insignia's dining room

A suggestive ambiance emerges from owner David Abes (formerly at the Horseradish Grill), Chef Pete Pavesic and General Manager Diedre Martin at their nouveau cuisine eatery on the edge of Buckhead. Signals of an eclectic menu subtly escape from the comforting mood. An array of wood fixtures, background chitchat, abstract artwork and dull lighting prevail. A juncture between a modern scene and a renovated loft. A unique aroma fills the air, embellishing a near memory, giving up a laugh or two. From the quiet environment, to the busy kitchen...

It's in the kitchen where the real ambiance unfolds at Insignia. Southwest flavors ... New American ... Continental specialties ... Los Angeles ... Old South ... Avant-garde ... Asian ... traveling the landscapes of food like a cross-cultural journey.

Crispy vegetable rolls with a sweet chili and cilantro sauce embark a move of sorts. A first bit suspends itself, until the last crumb — complicated, yet evolving slowly. Nearly akin, a combination of lightly sauteéd onions, satoki, snowpeas, yellow cumin and fresh green turmeric, trailing a hint of coconut milk.

From land and air is offered the spit roasted French pork chops with vanilla sweet potatoes and a plum glaze. Or pan roasted maple leaf farm duck breast with a wild mushroom and herb roasted cous cous, shaved asparagus and walnuts with a winter citrus sauce.

Conjuring up delicacies from rivers, lakes and oceans, a compliment of steamed black mussels in Asian bouillabaisse gravitates a soujourn. The grilled tuna over spinach infused mashed potatoes and a pinot noir sauce offers insight into the signature style as a rumor emerges in the background: "Those potatoes are made in heaven." Almost redemptive was the Pacific Rim style Hawaiian fish — sake kasu over jasmine rice and stir-fried vegetables.

Settling matters wasn't as difficult as anticipated. Seconding an emotion was a delicate presentation of the créme brulée. Crisply wafers donning a complex, immaculate créme are enhanced with strawberry tastes.

With the alluring ambiance, the restaurant's signature beckons; with the intricate flavors, the insignia is inscribed.

Lunch and Dinner
Small Plates: $5-$12; Entreés: $13-26
Dinner for two with white/red wine: $45.60

Insignia
4279 Roswell Rd. Suite 103
(404) 256-4040
www.insigniacuisine.com

Guillaume
Young heart
Jeune
Old Soul
Bill Sweeney